Dracula,
motherf*ker!

by

Alex de Campi
Erica Henderson

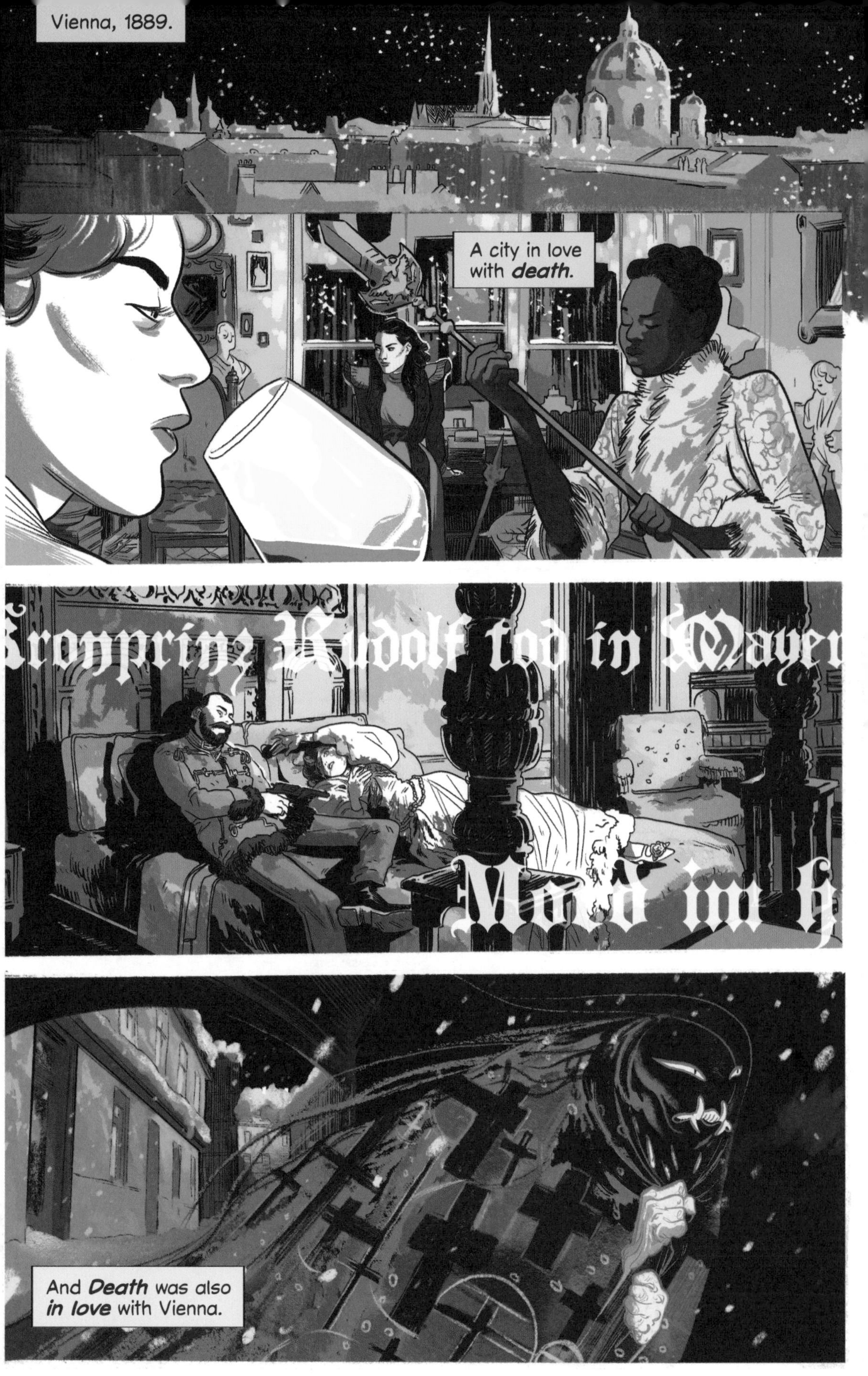
Vienna, 1889.
A city in love with *death*.
And *Death* was also *in love* with Vienna.

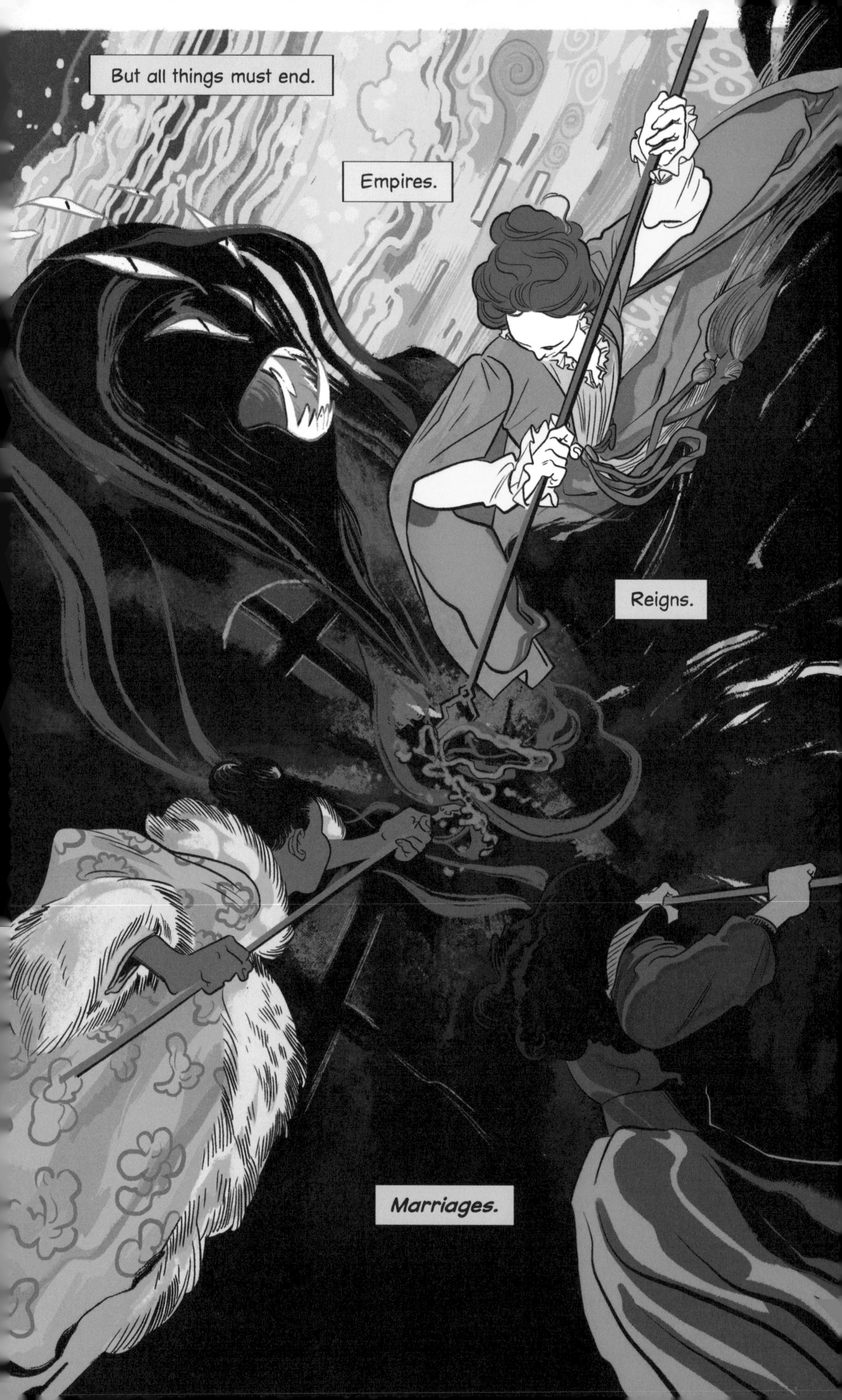
But all things must end.
Empires.
Reigns.
Marriages.

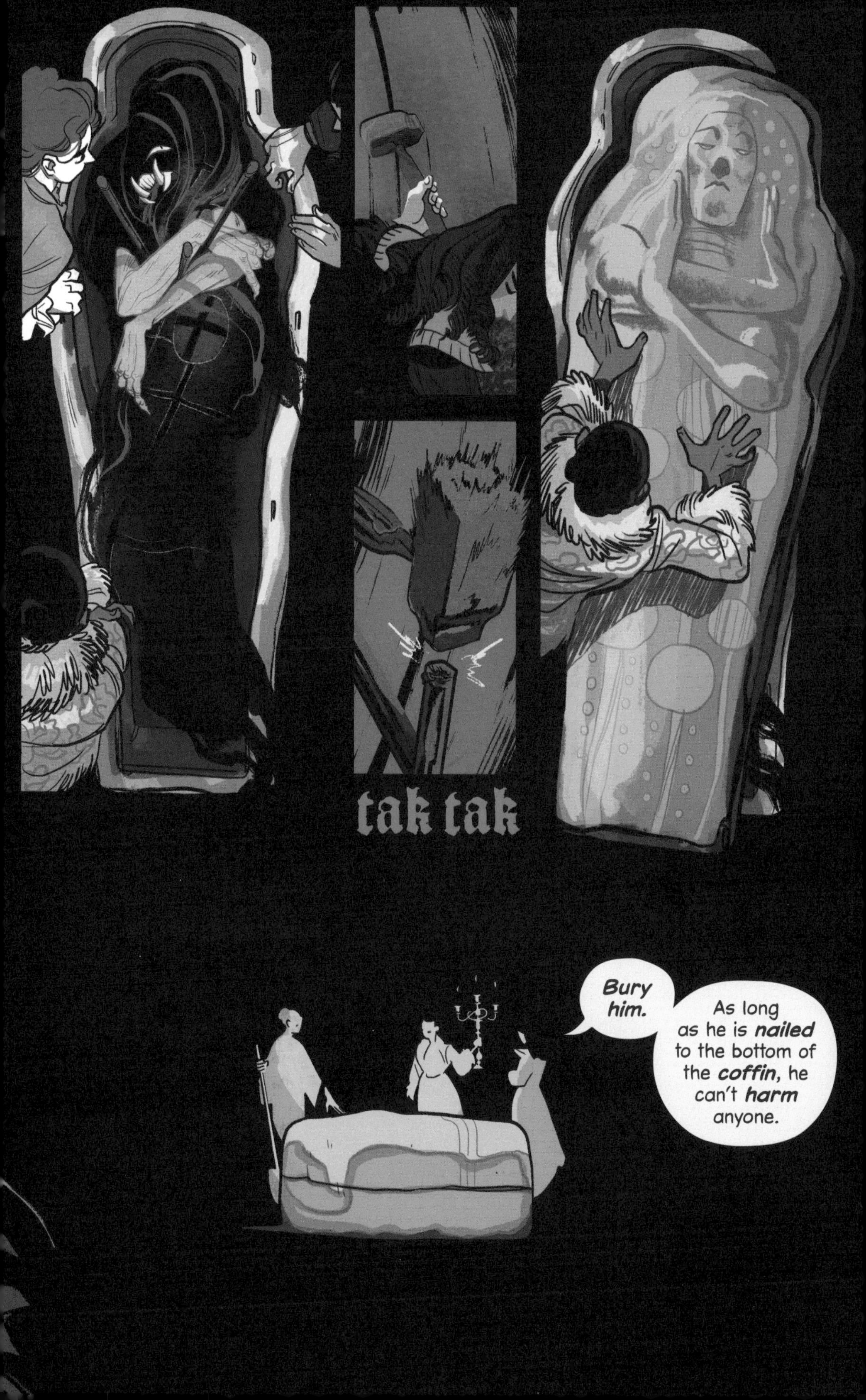
tak tak
Bury him.
As long as he is nailed to the bottom of the coffin, he can't harm anyone.

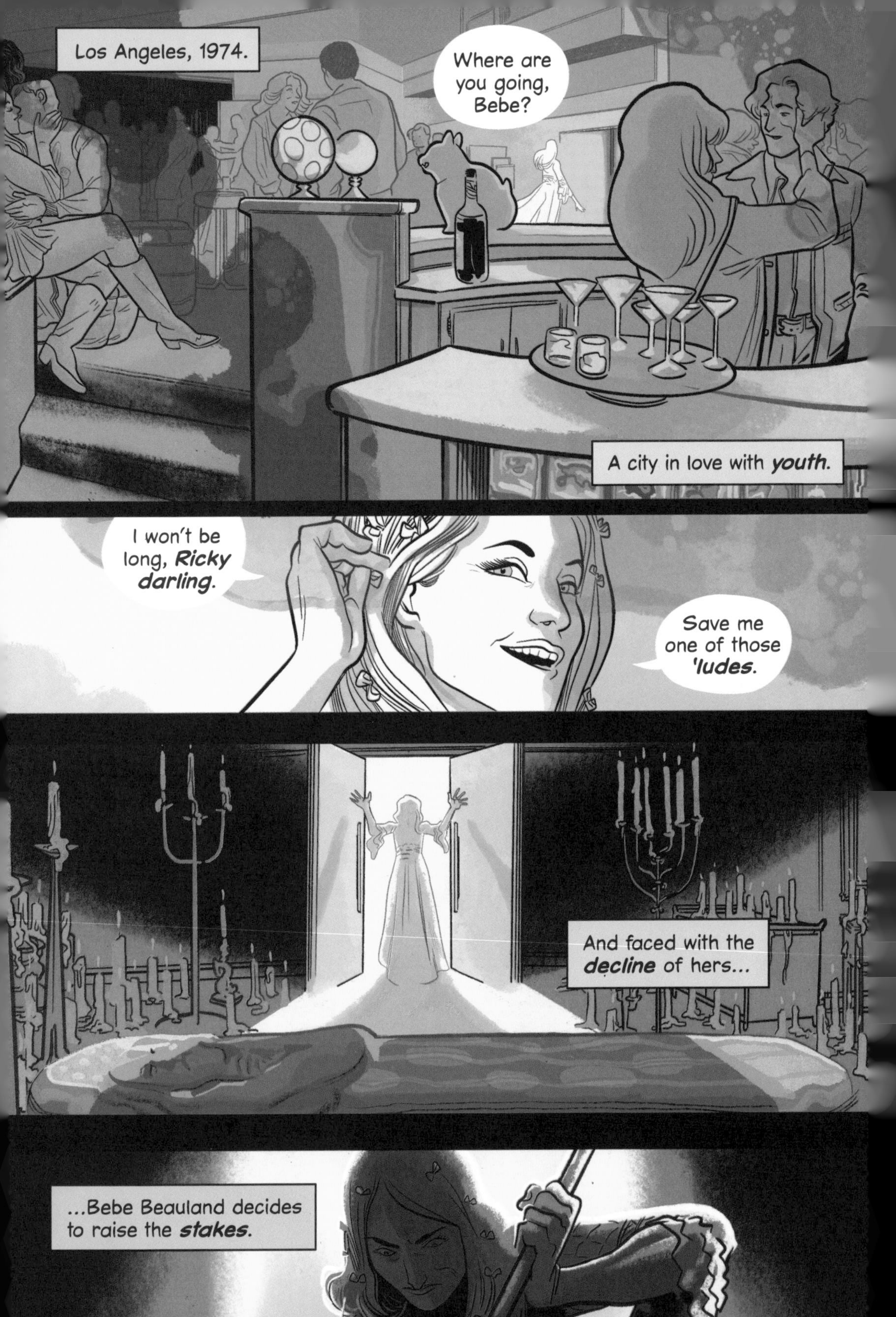

Los Angeles, 1974.
Where are you going, Bebe?
A city in love with *youth*.
I won't be long, *Ricky darling*.
Save me one of those *'ludes*.
And faced with the *decline* of hers...
...Bebe Beauland decides to raise the *stakes*.

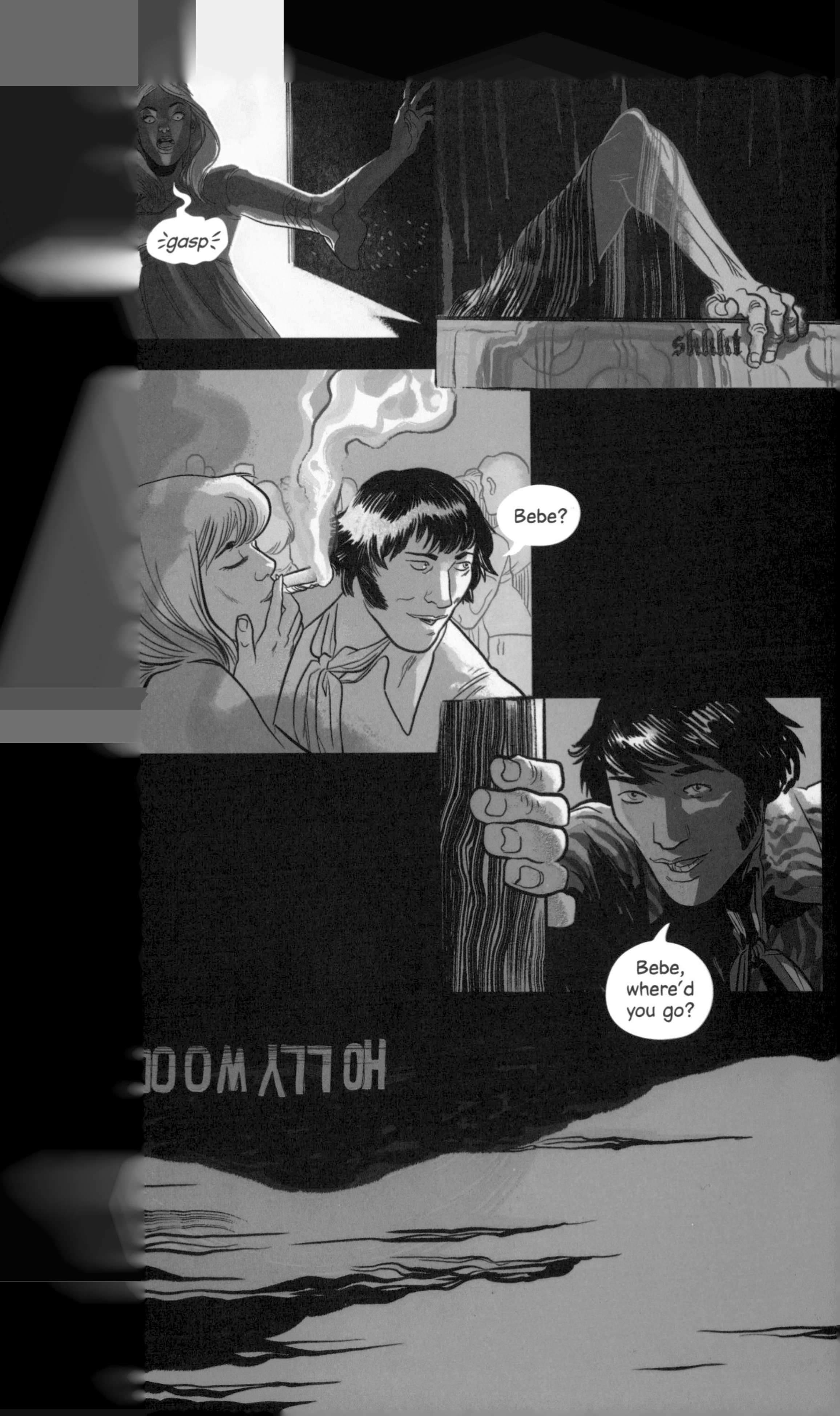
gasp
shhht
Bebe?
Bebe, where'd you go?

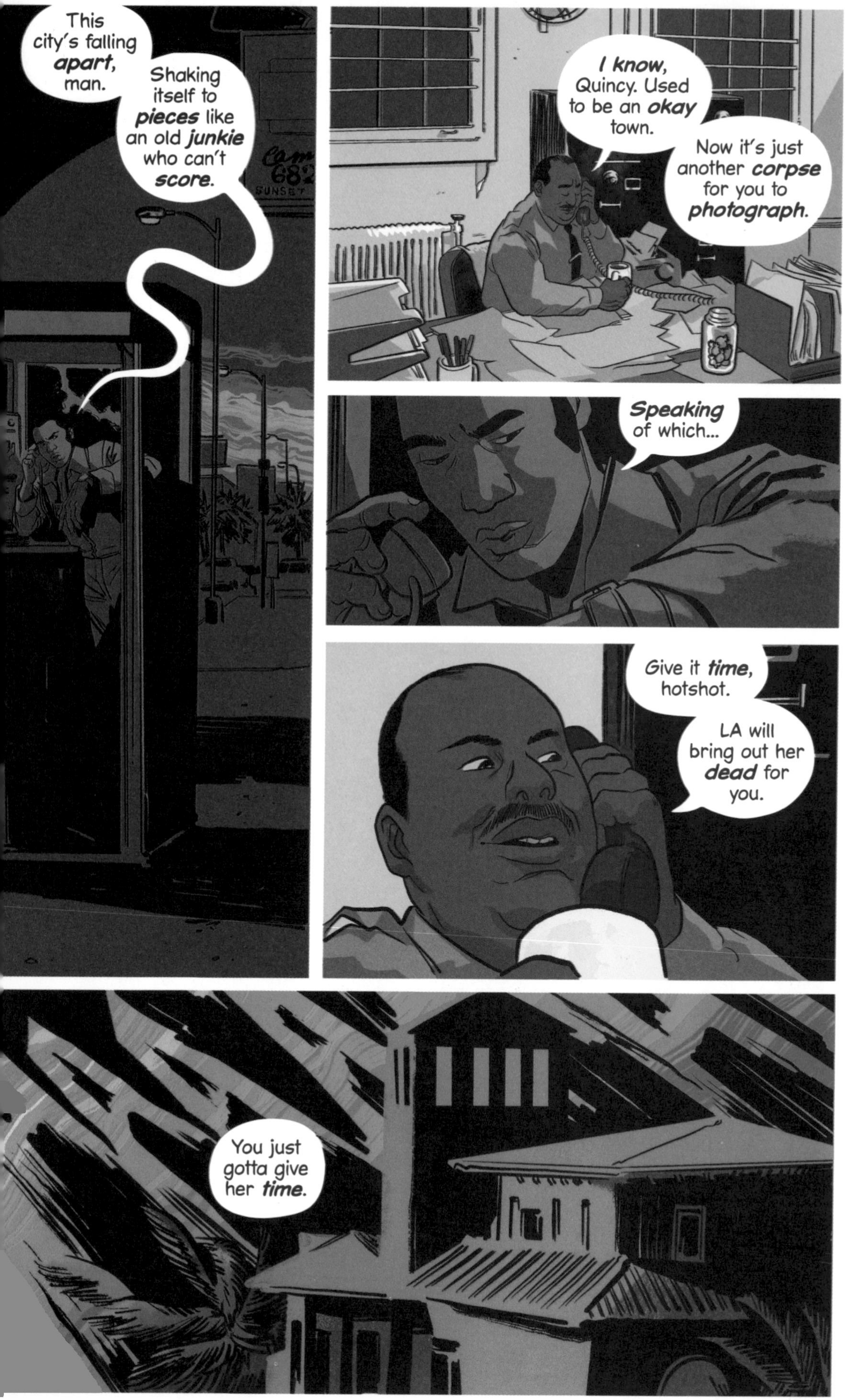
This city's falling apart, man.
Shaking itself to pieces like an old junkie who can't score.
I know, Quincy. Used to be an okay town.
Now it's just another corpse for you to photograph.
Speaking of which...
Give it time, hotshot.
LA will bring out her dead for you.
You just gotta give her time.

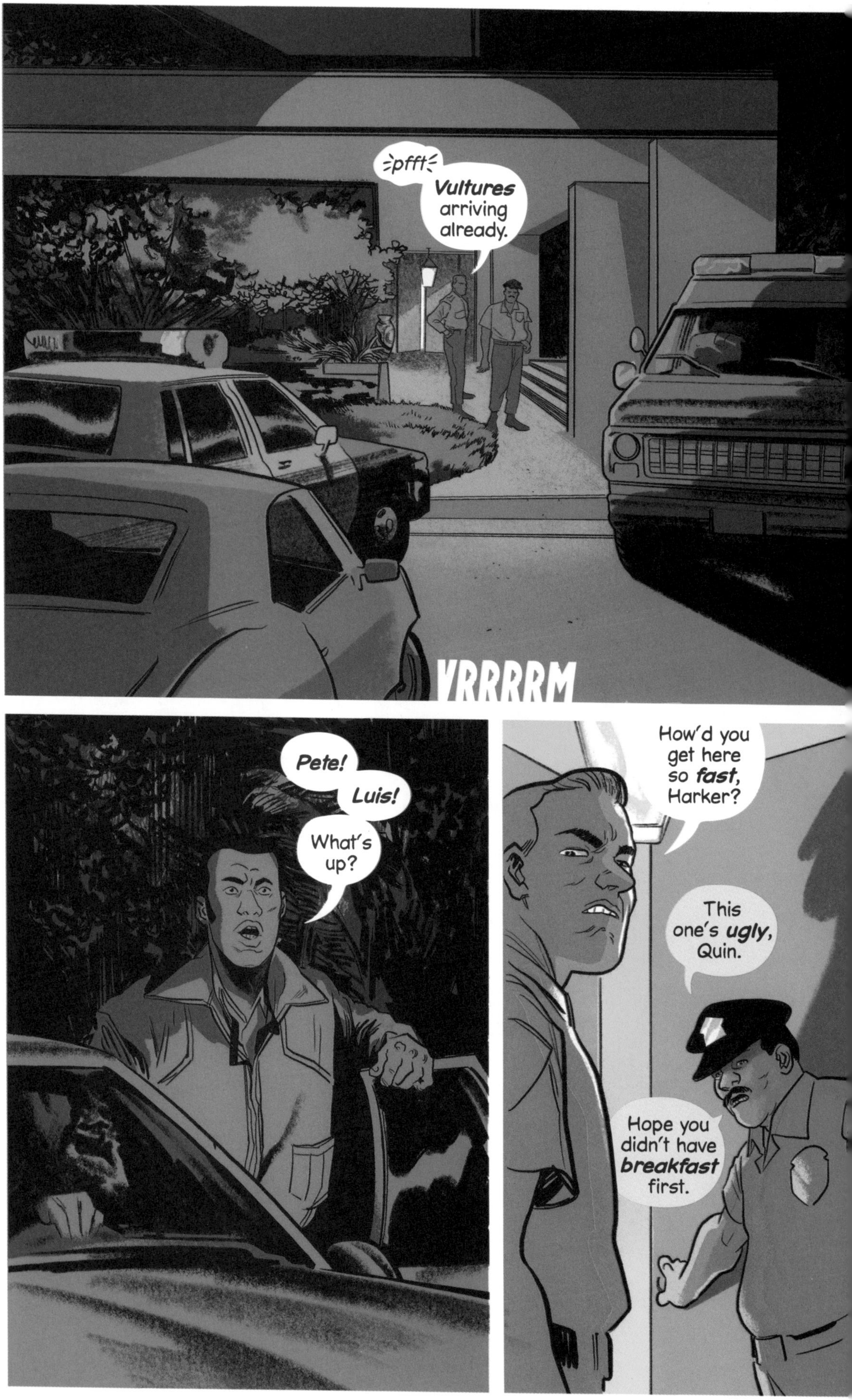

pfft
Vultures arriving already.
VRRRRM
Pete!
Luis!
What's up?
How'd you get here so fast, Harker?
This one's ugly, Quin.
Hope you didn't have breakfast first.

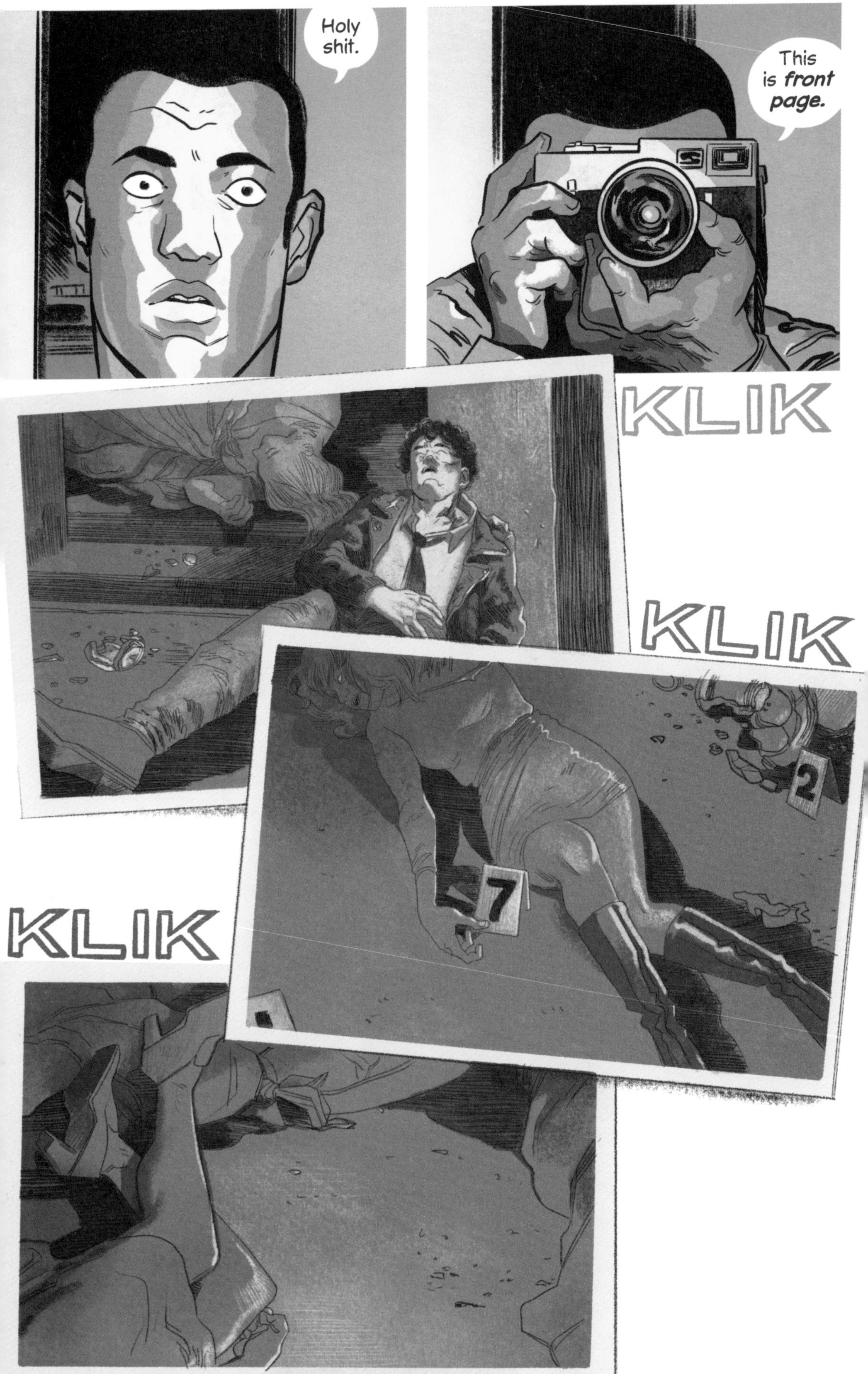
Holy shit.
This is *front page.*
KLIK
KLIK
KLIK

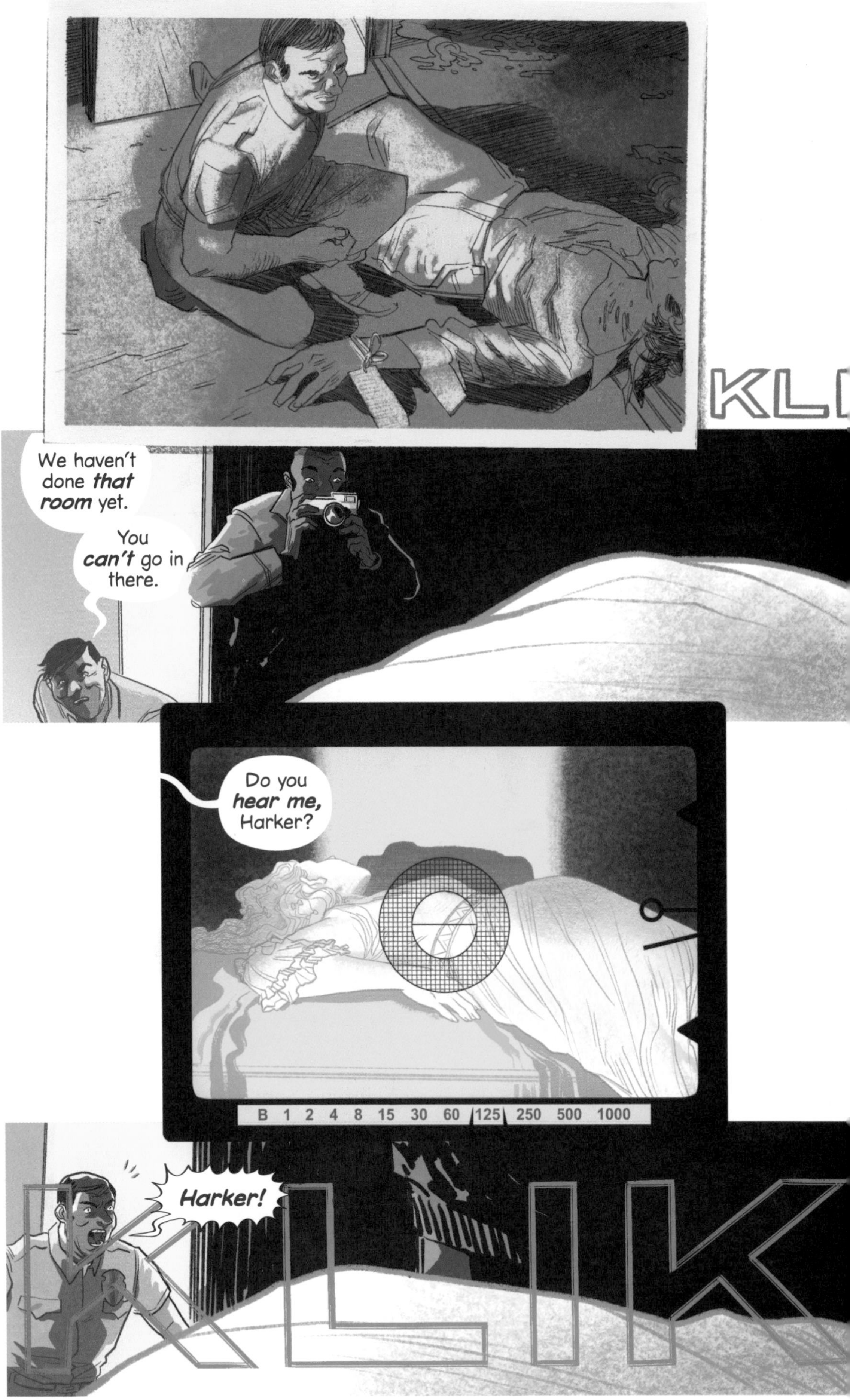
KLI
We haven't done ***that room*** yet.
You ***can't*** go in there.
Do you ***hear me,*** Harker?
B 1 2 4 8 15 30 60 125 250 500 1000
Harker!
KLIK

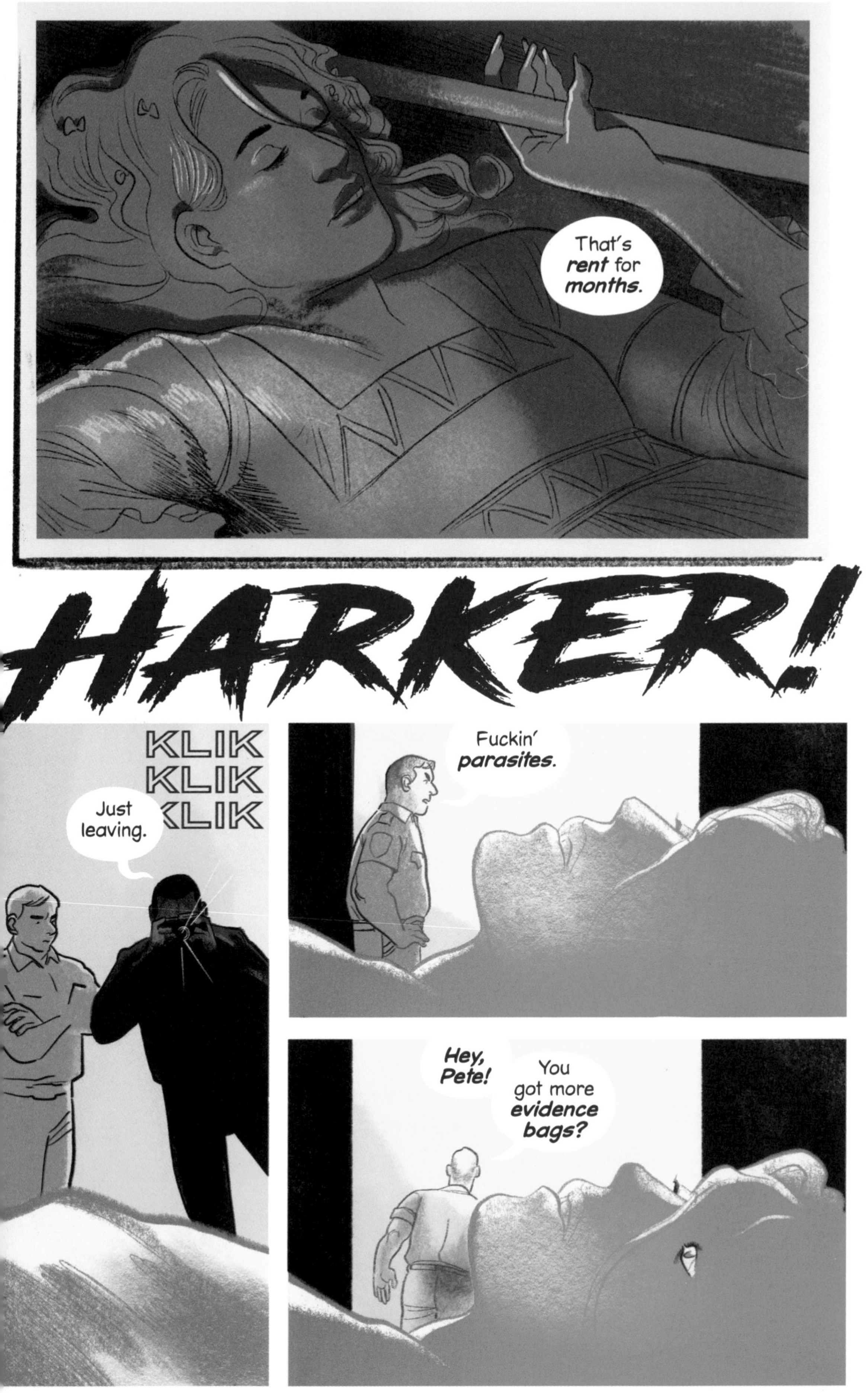

That's *rent* for *months.*
HARKER!
KLIK KLIK KLIK
Just leaving.
Fuckin' *parasites.*
Hey, Pete!
You got more *evidence bags?*

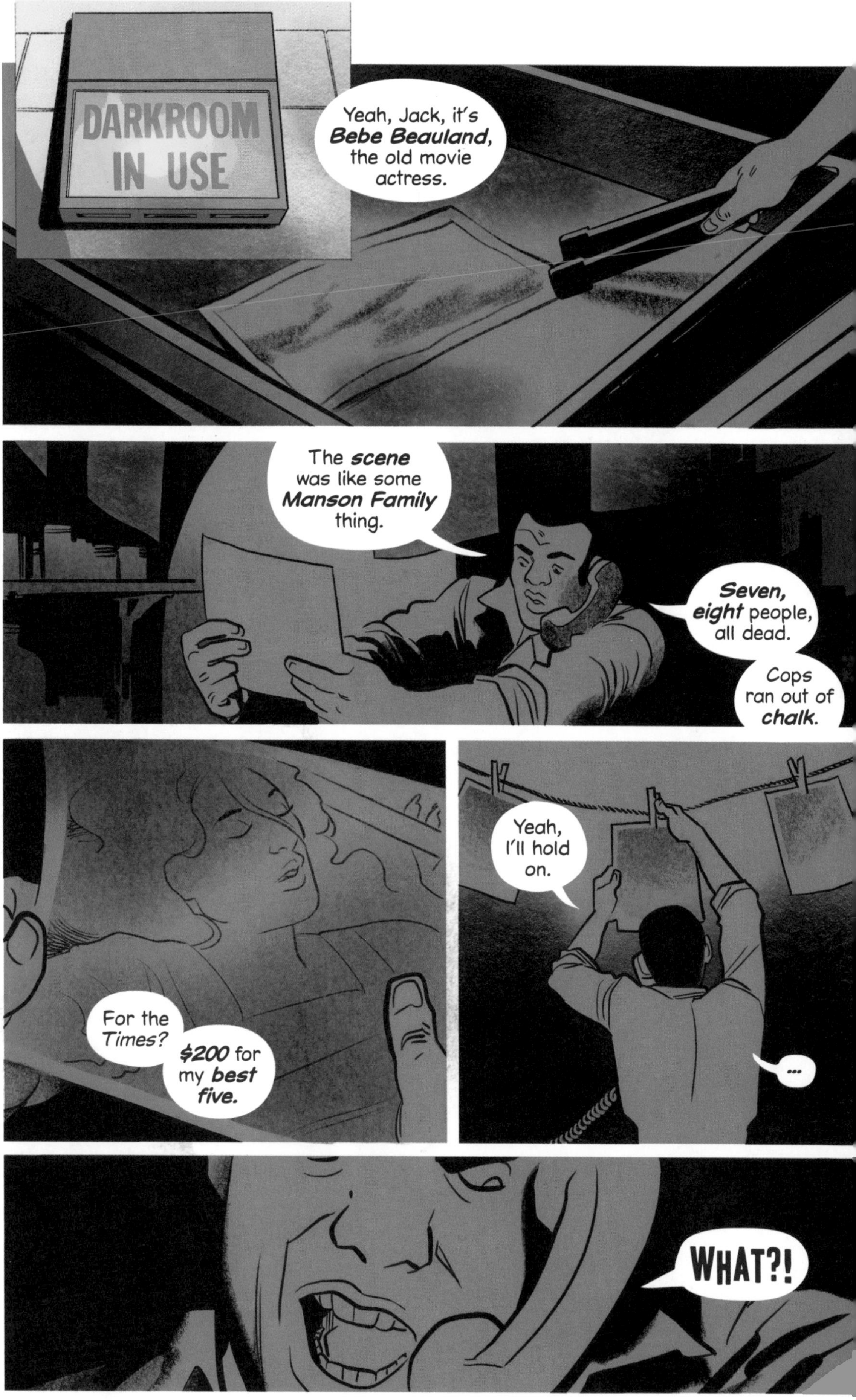
DARKROOM IN USE
Yeah, Jack, it's *Bebe Beauland,* the old movie actress.
The *scene* was like some *Manson Family* thing.
Seven, eight people, all dead.
Cops ran out of *chalk.*
For the *Times?*
$200 for my *best five.*
Yeah, I'll hold on.
...
WHAT?!

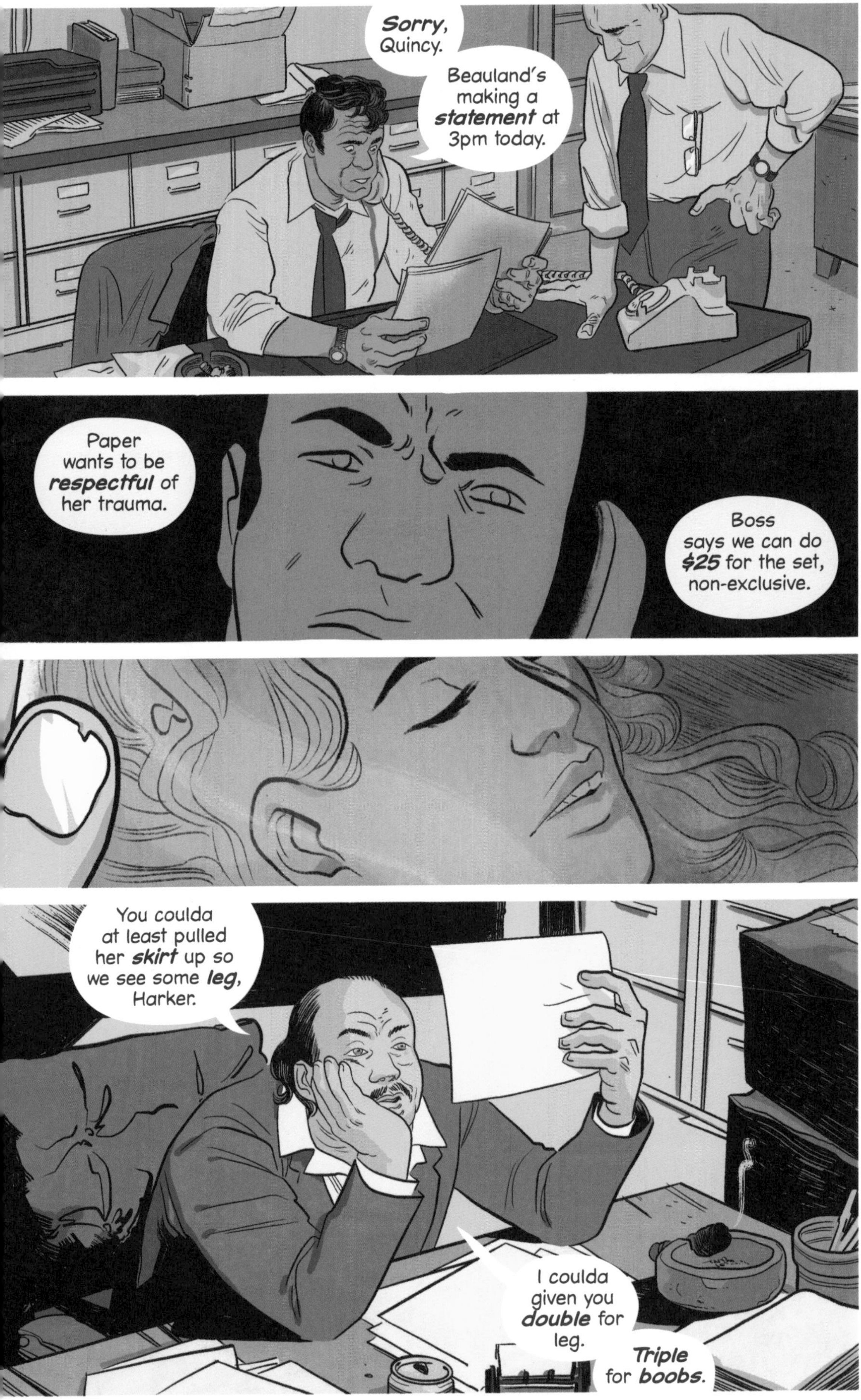

Sorry, Quincy.
Beauland's making a ***statement*** at 3pm today.
Paper wants to be ***respectful*** of her trauma.
Boss says we can do ***$25*** for the set, non-exclusive.
You coulda at least pulled her ***skirt*** up so we see some ***leg,*** Harker.
I coulda given you ***double*** for leg.
Triple for ***boobs.***

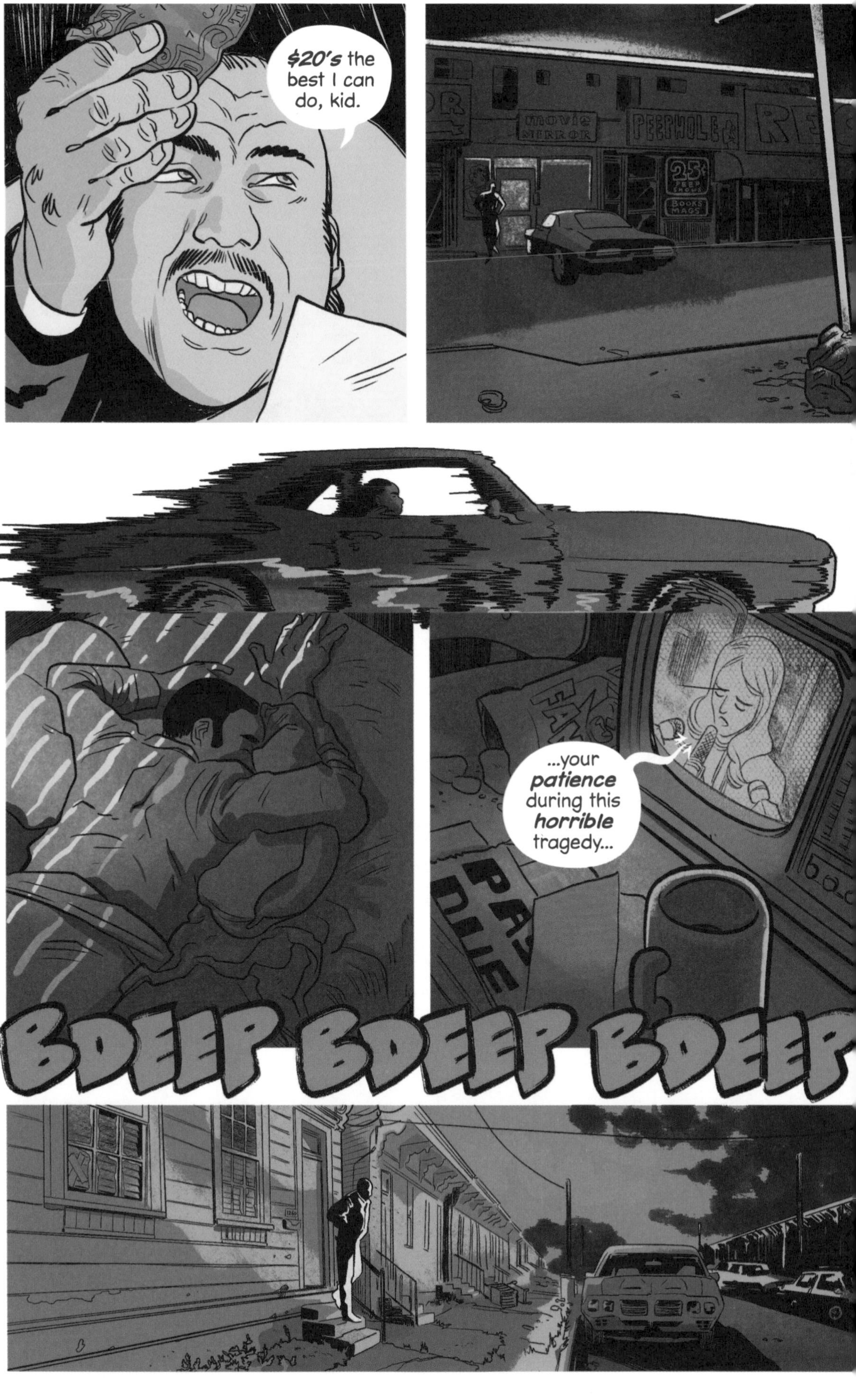
$20's the best I can do, kid.
movie MIRROR
PEEPHOLE
25¢
BOOKS MAGS
...your patience during this horrible tragedy...
BDEEP BDEEP BDEEP

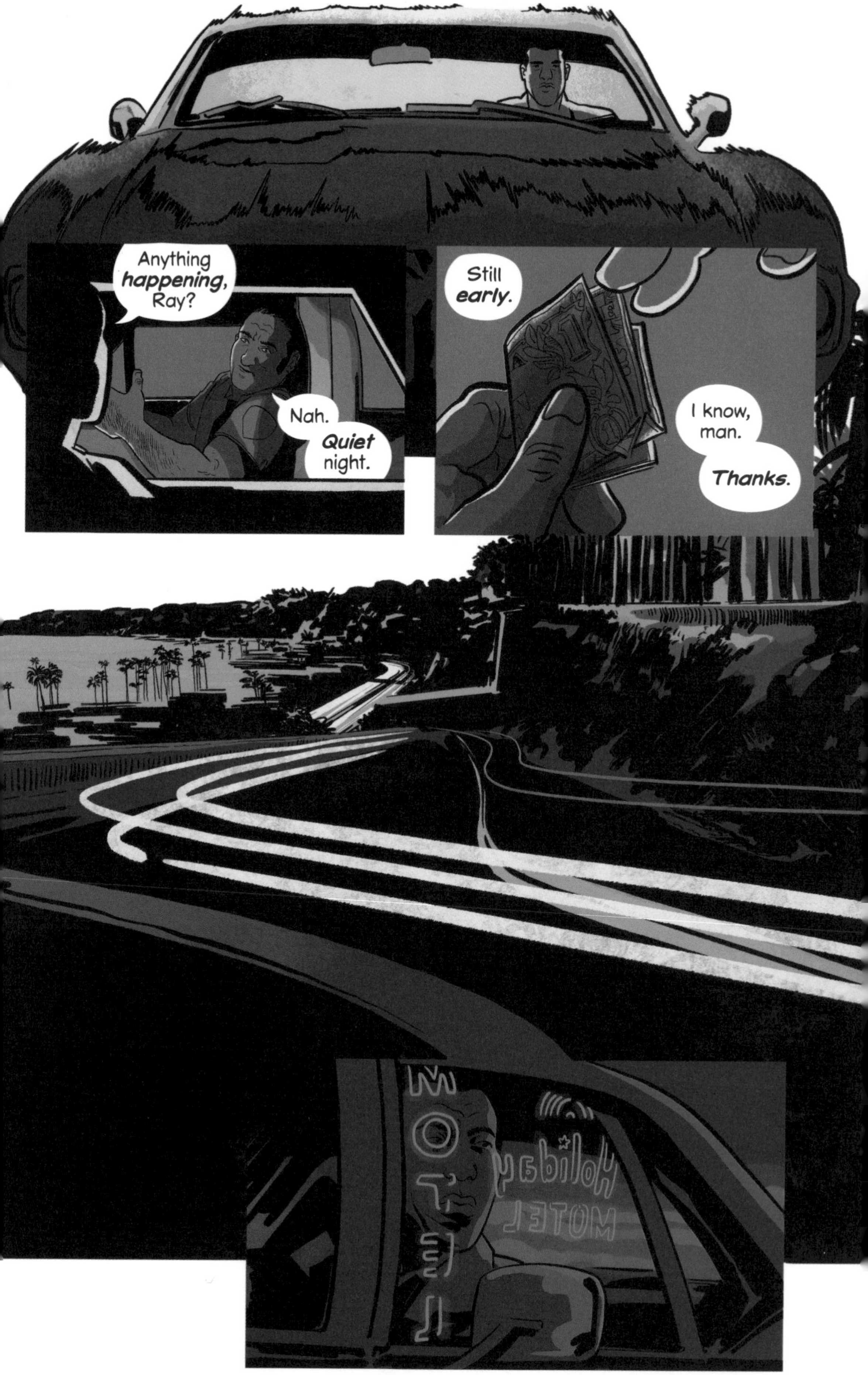
Anything happening, Ray?
Nah. Quiet night.
Still early.
I know, man.
Thanks.
MOTEL
Holiday MOTEL

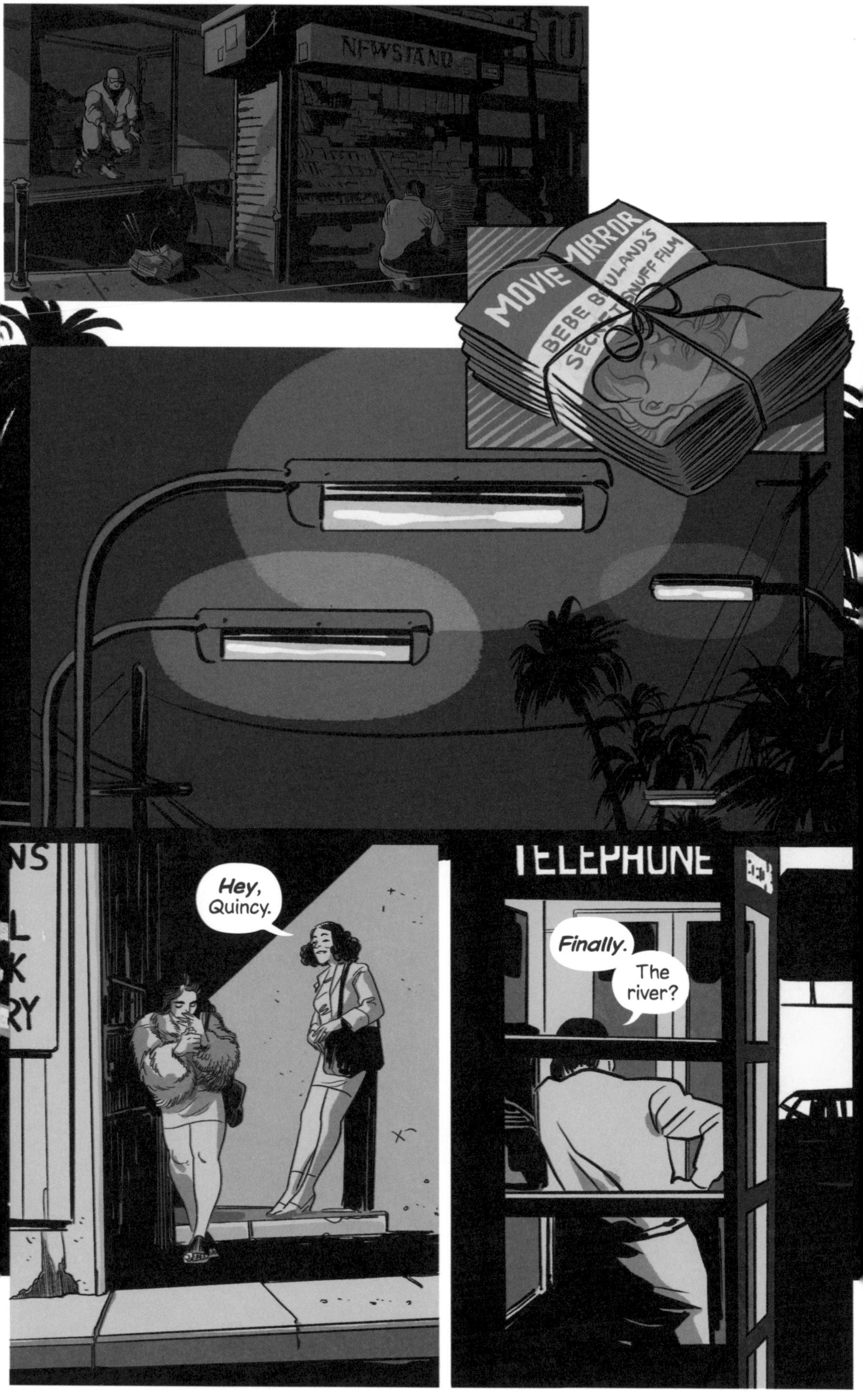
NEWSTAND
MOVIE MIRROR
SNUFF FILM
Hey, Quincy.
TELEPHONE
Finally.
The river?

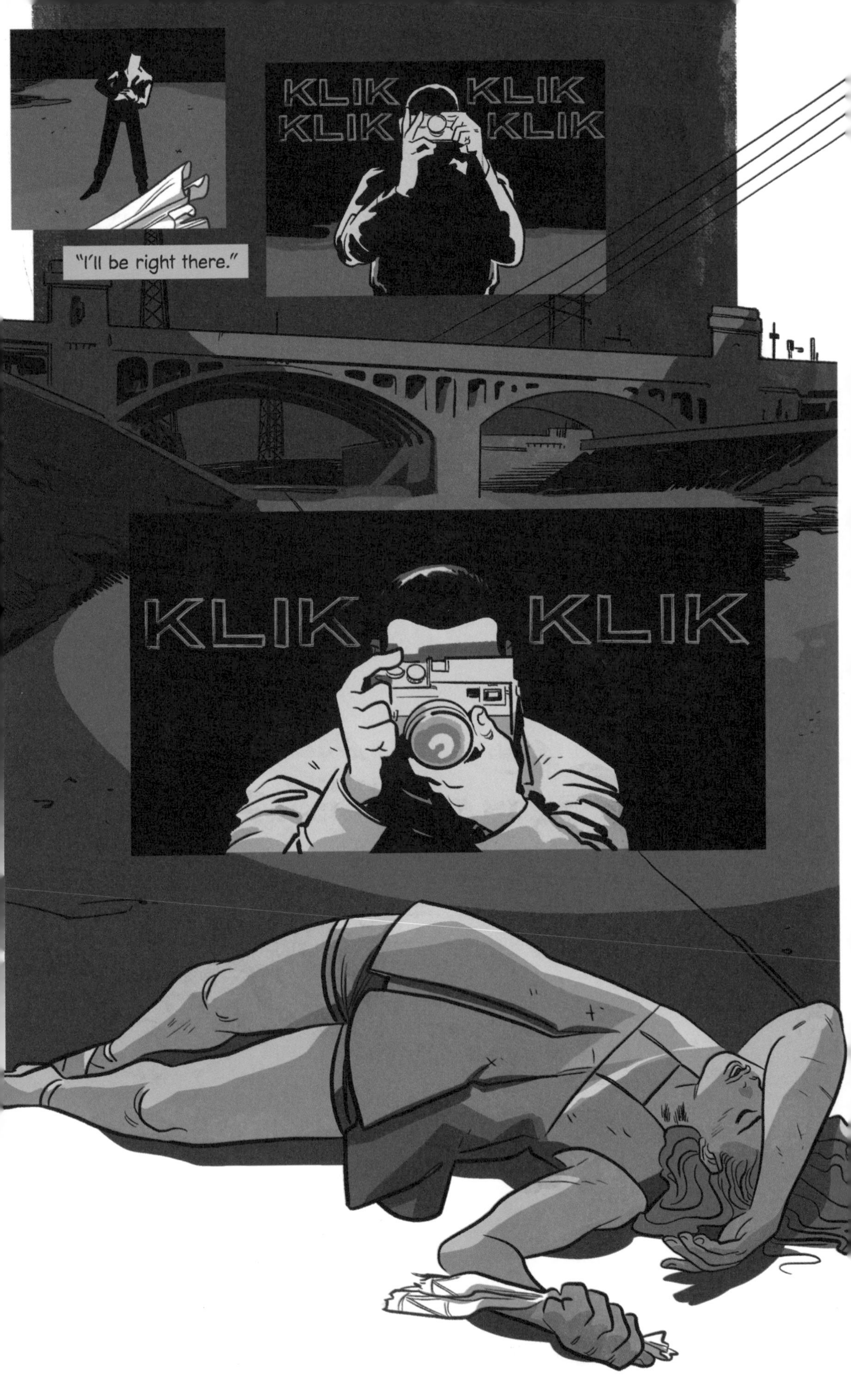
"I'll be right there."
KLIK KLIK
KLIK KLIK
KLIK KLIK

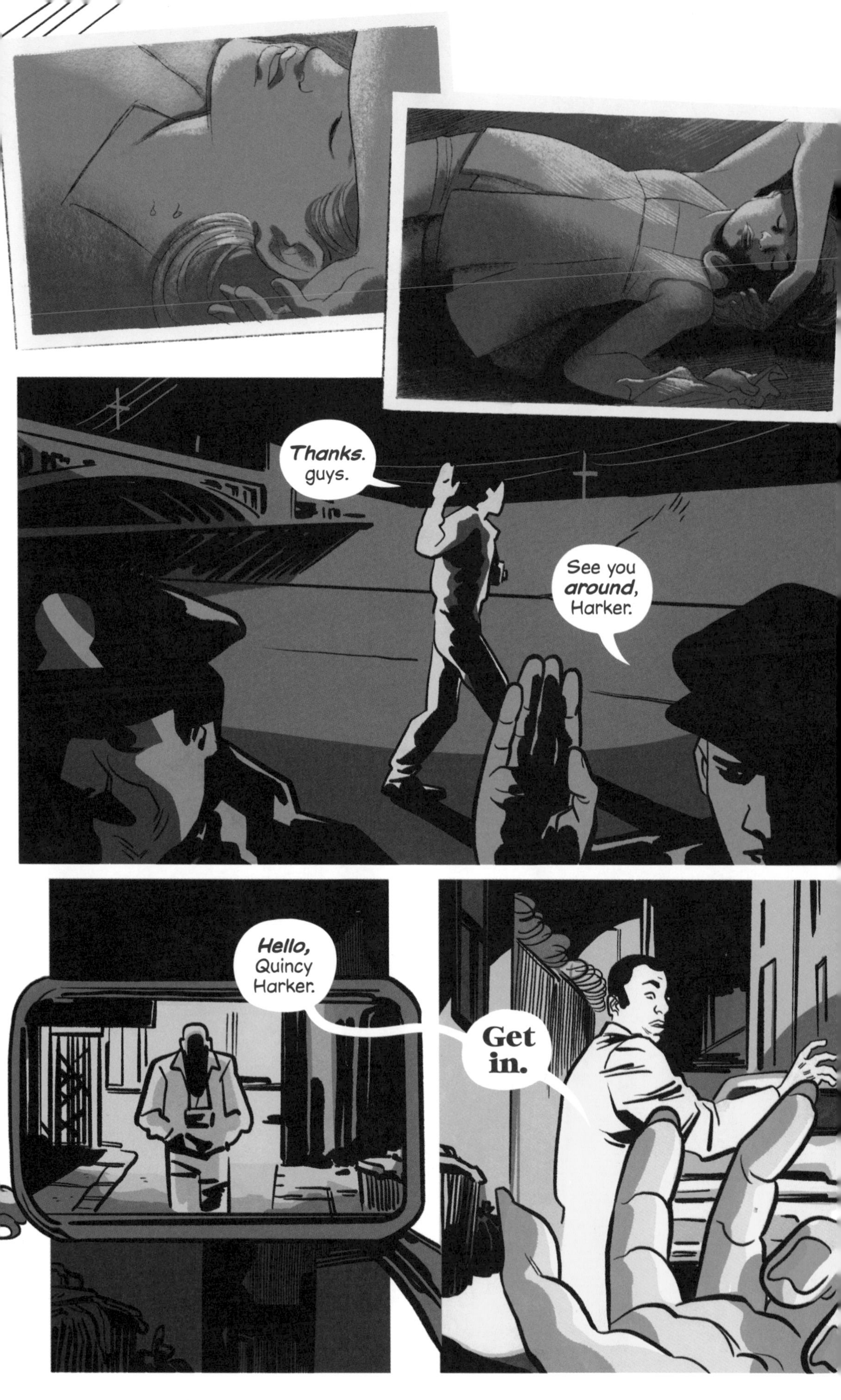
Thanks. guys.
See you around, Harker.
Hello, Quincy Harker.
Get in.

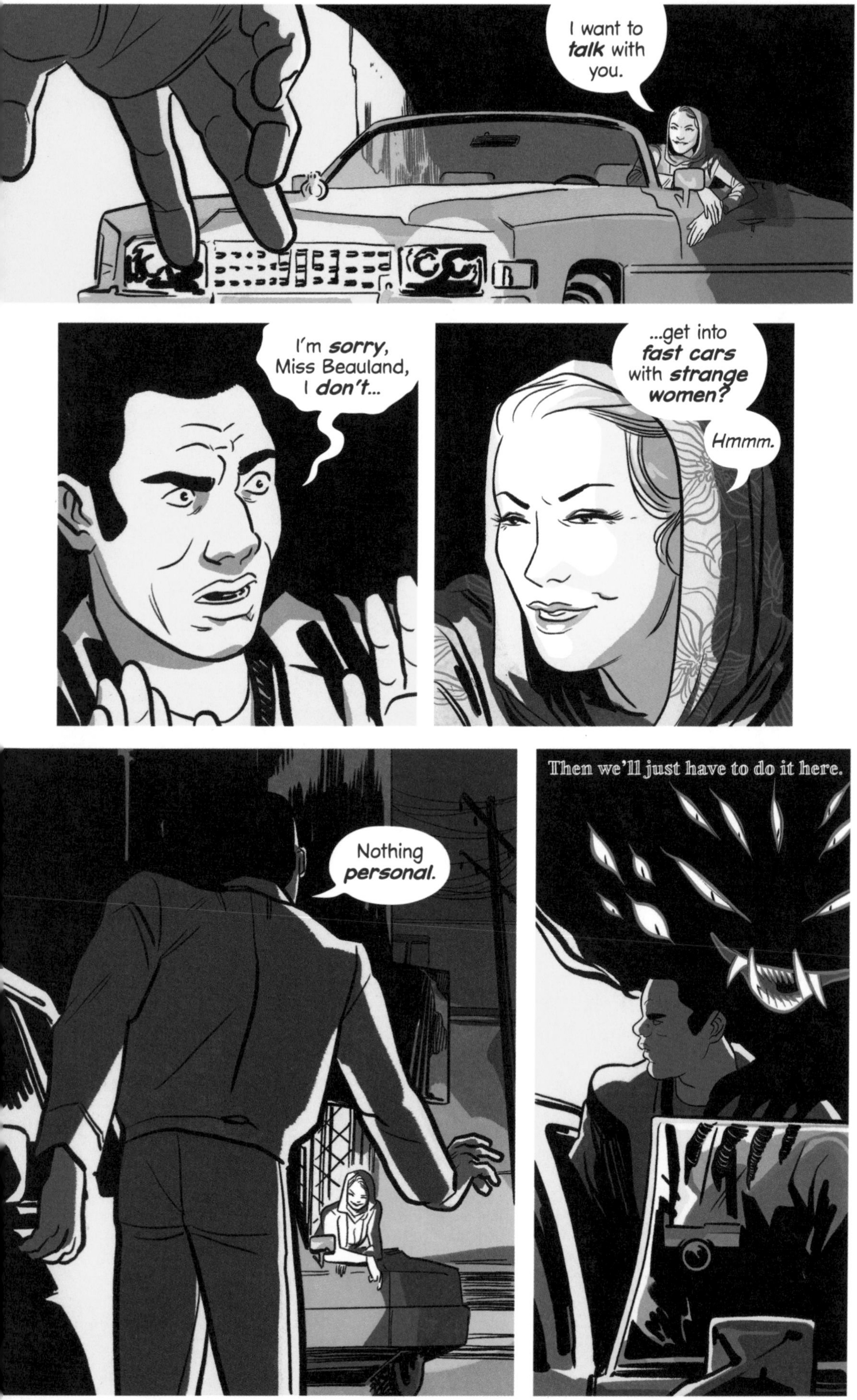

I want to *talk* with you.
I'm ***sorry***, Miss Beauland, I ***don't***...
...get into ***fast cars*** with ***strange women?***
Hmmm.
Nothing ***personal.***
Then we'll just have to do it here.

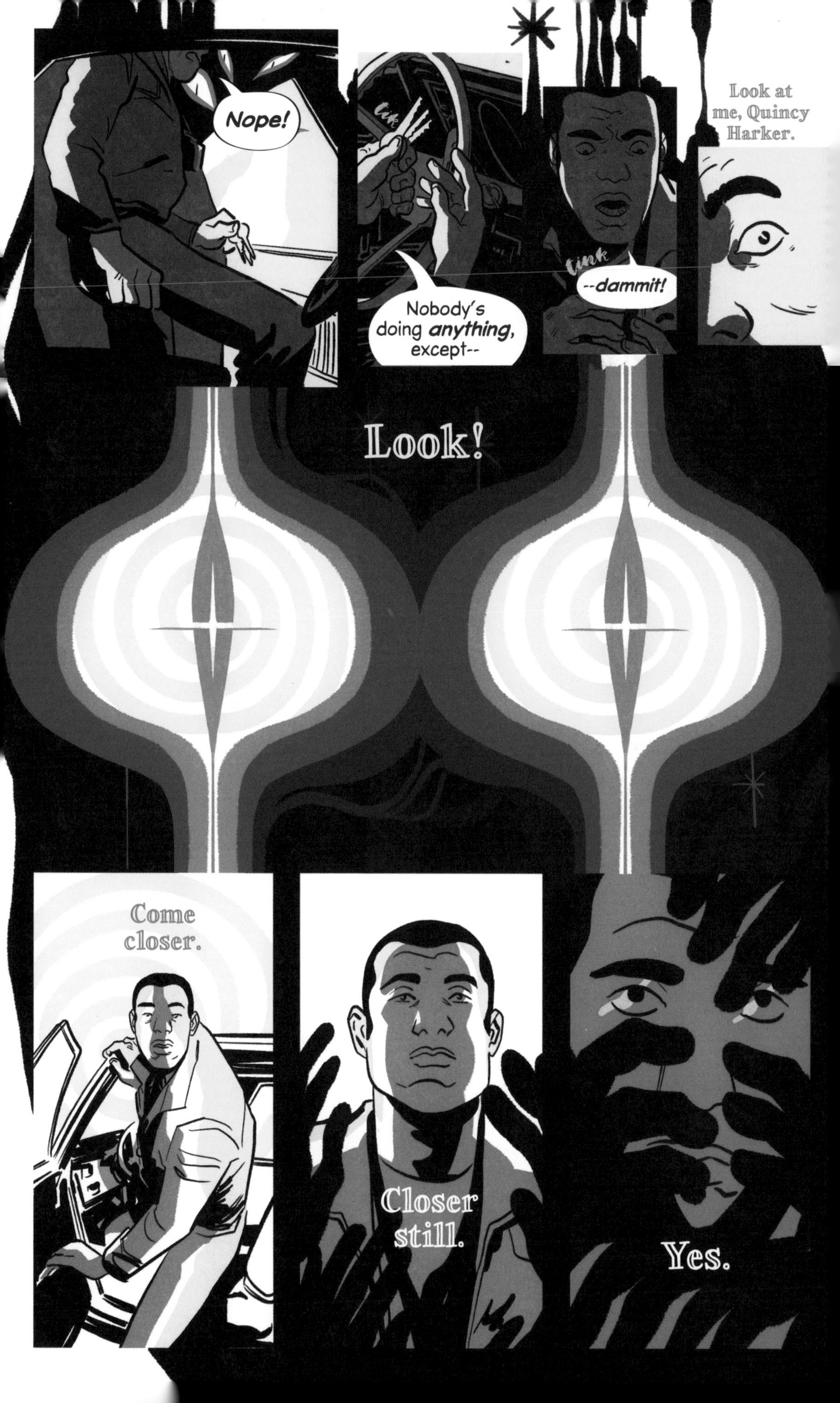
Nope!
tink
Nobody's doing *anything*, except--
tink
--dammit!
Look at me, Quincy Harker.
Look!
Come closer.
Closer still.
Yes.

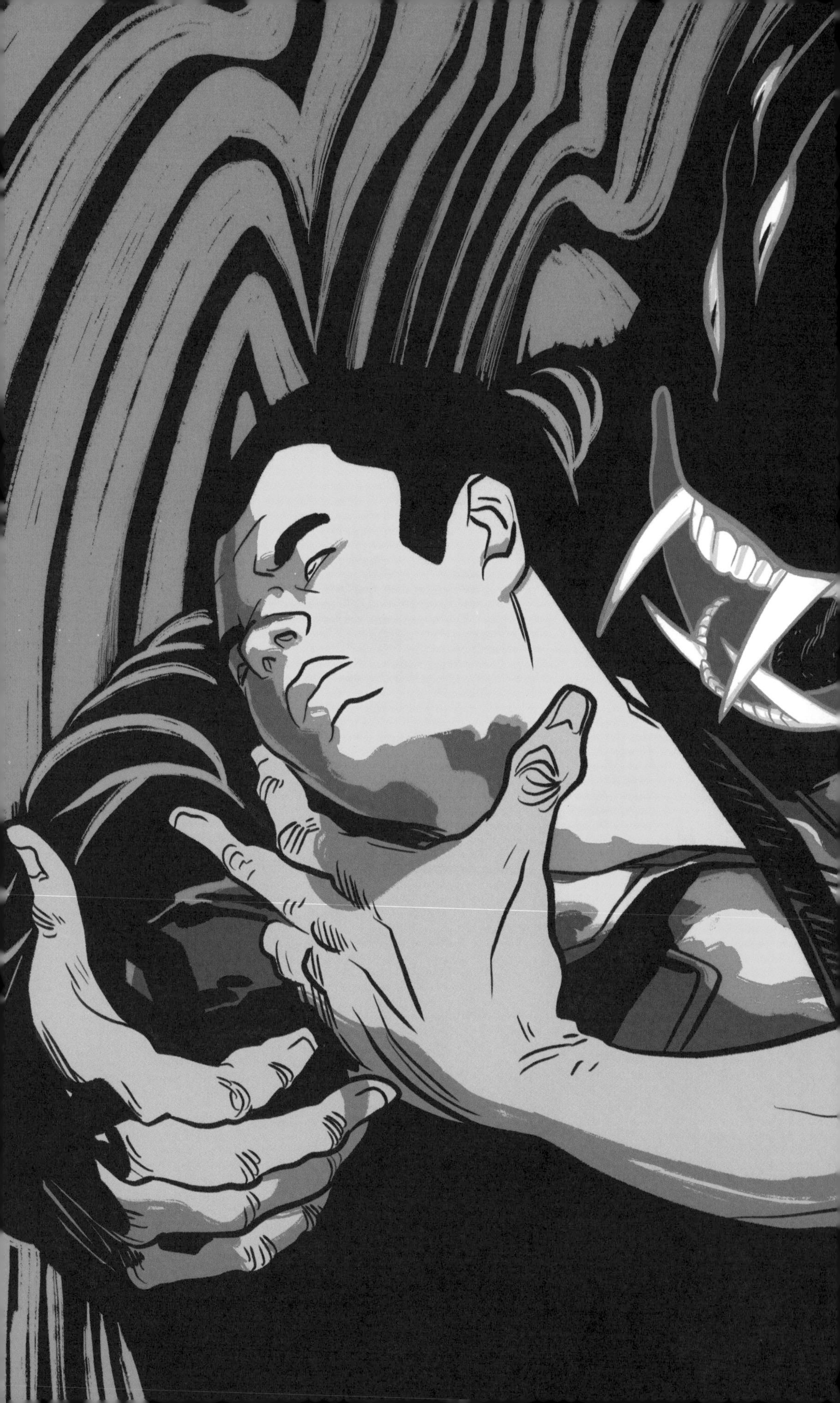

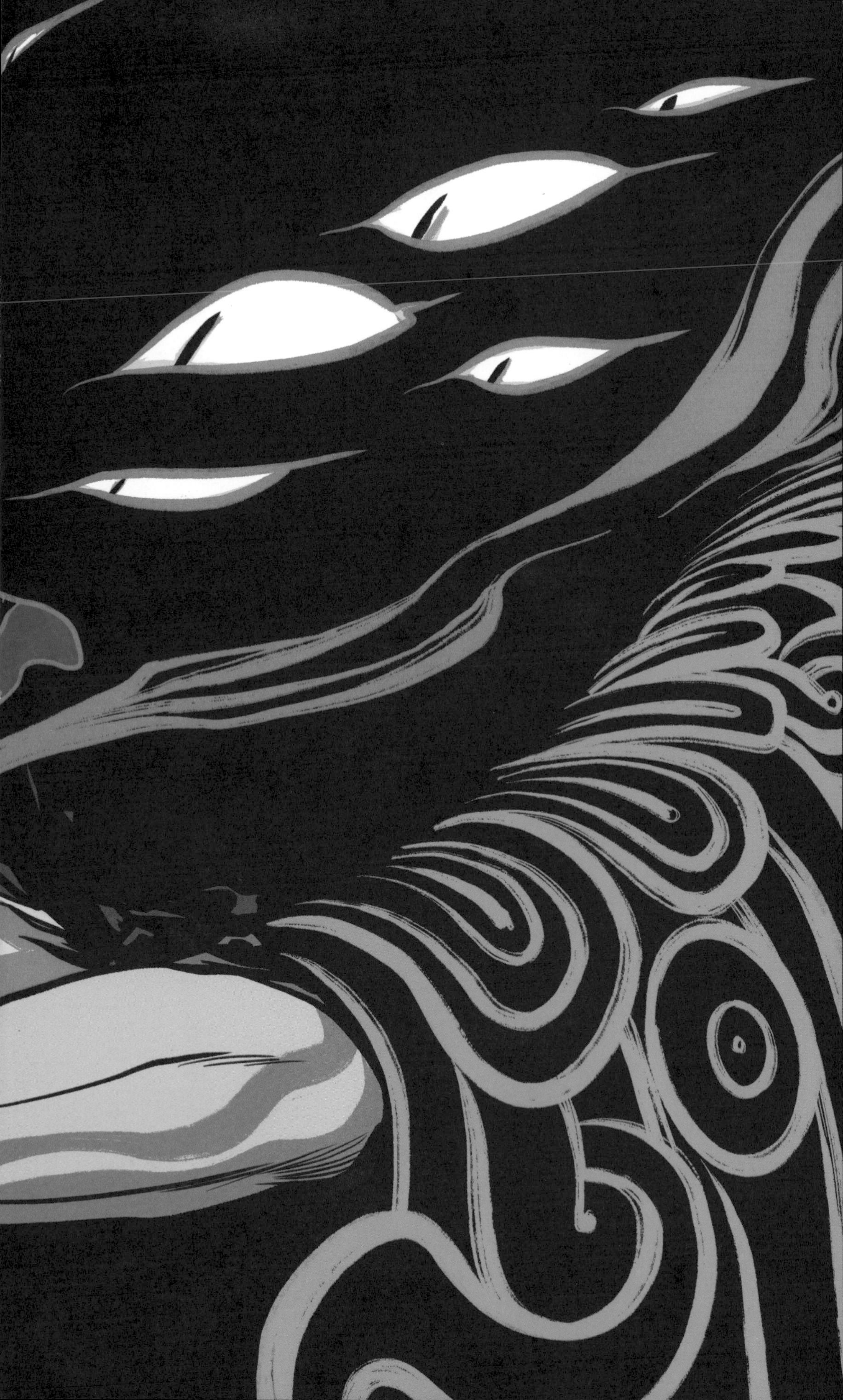

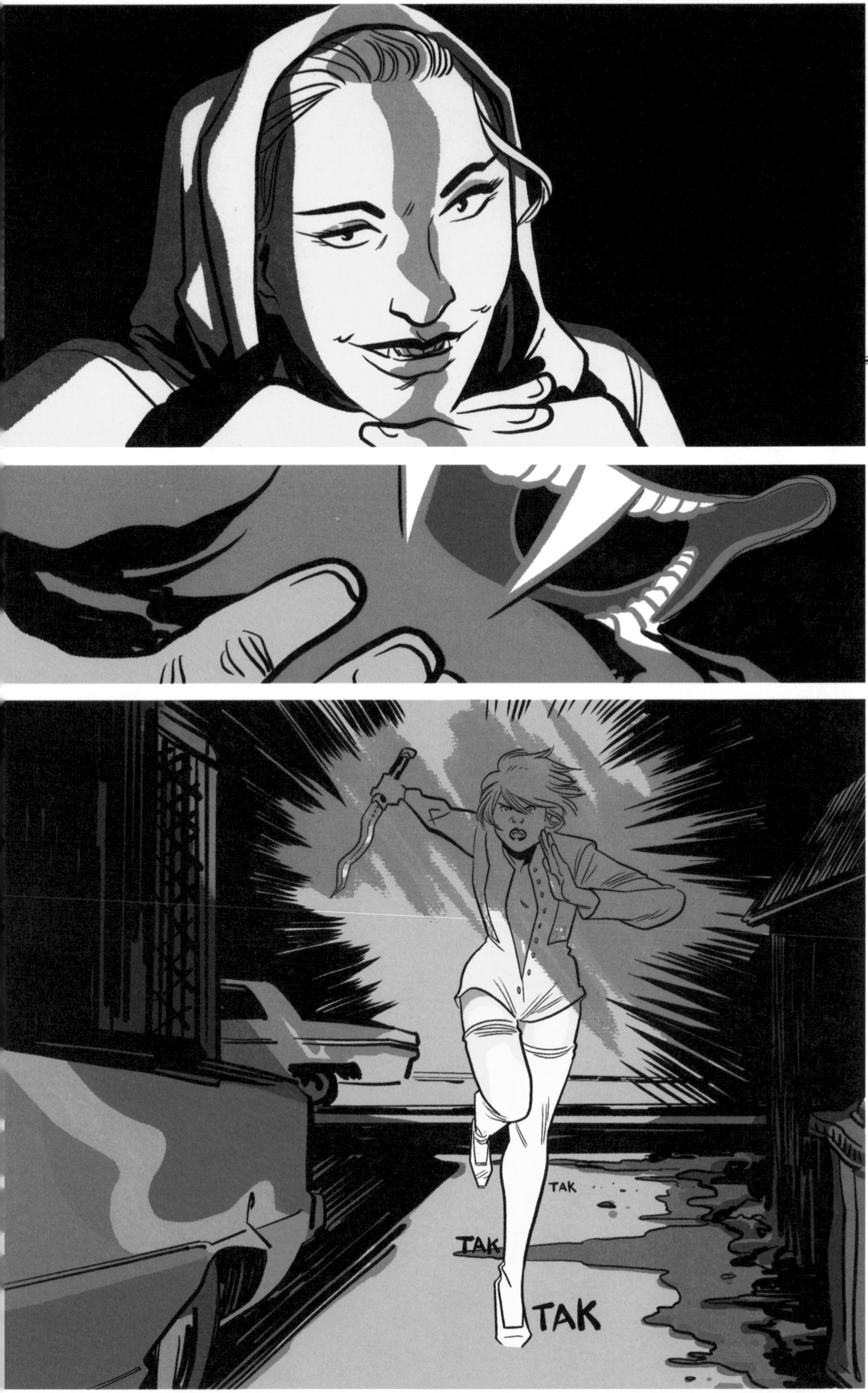
TAK
TAK
TAK

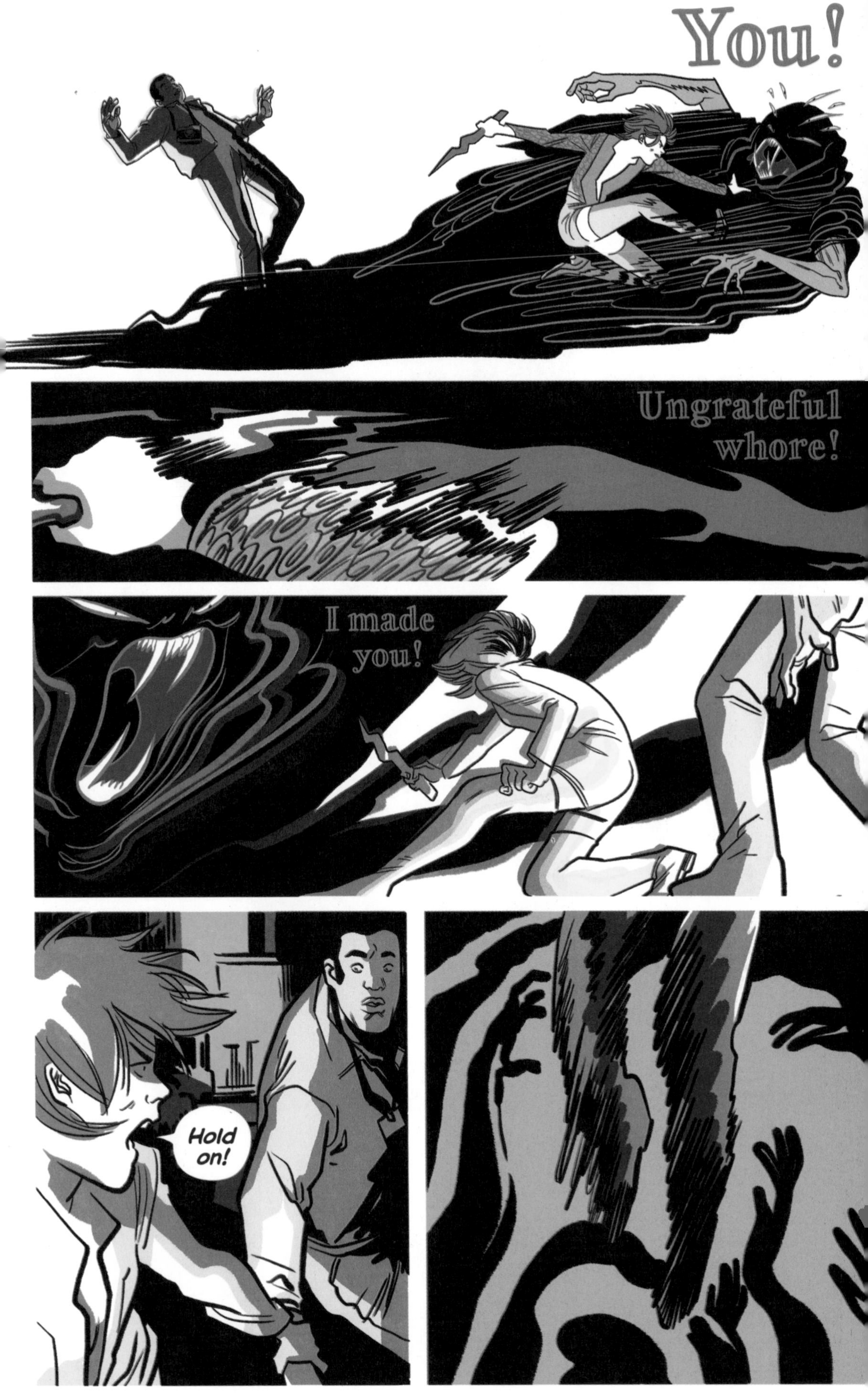
You!
Ungrateful whore!
I made you!
Hold on!

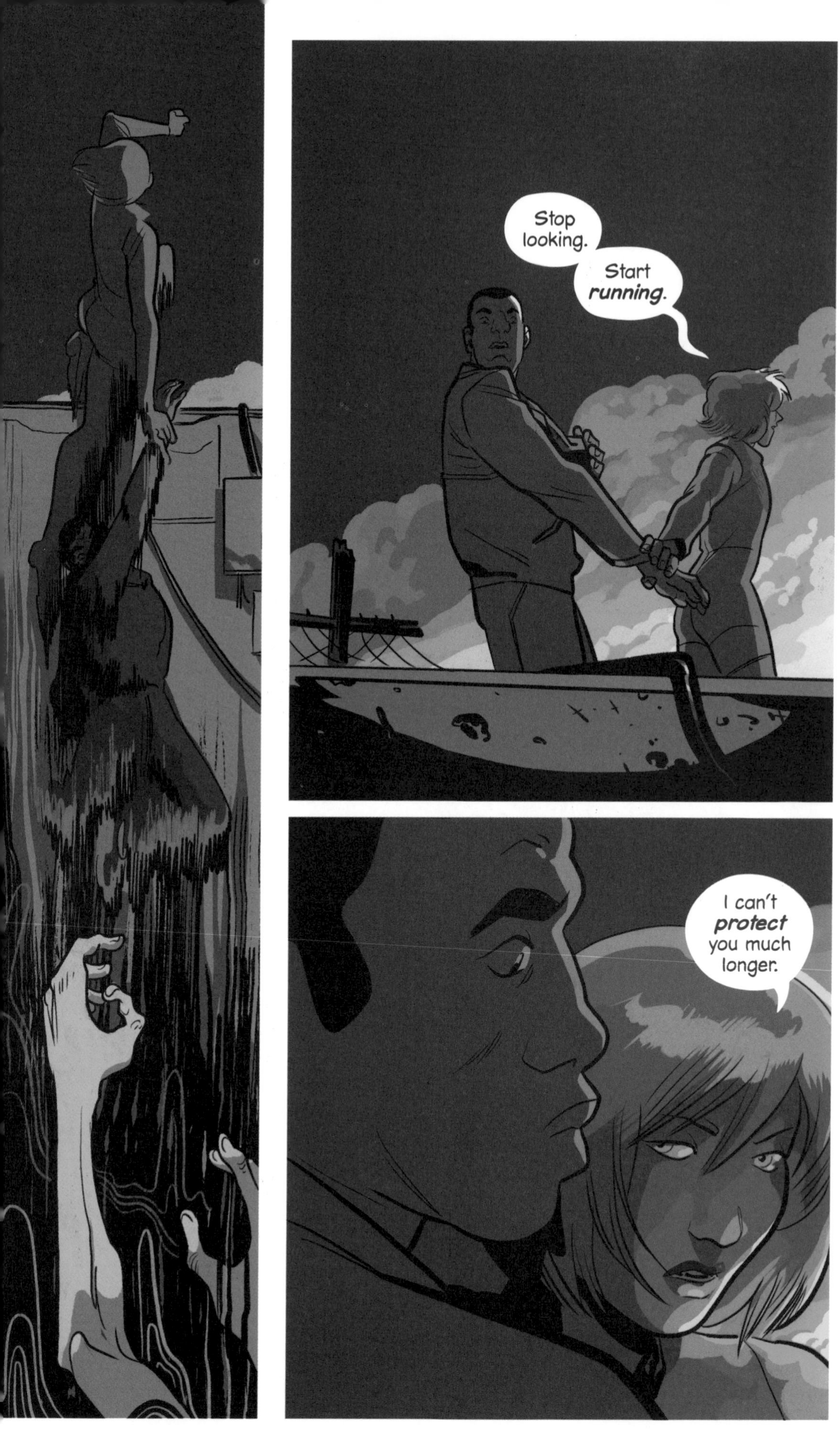
Stop looking.
Start *running*.
I can't *protect* you much longer.

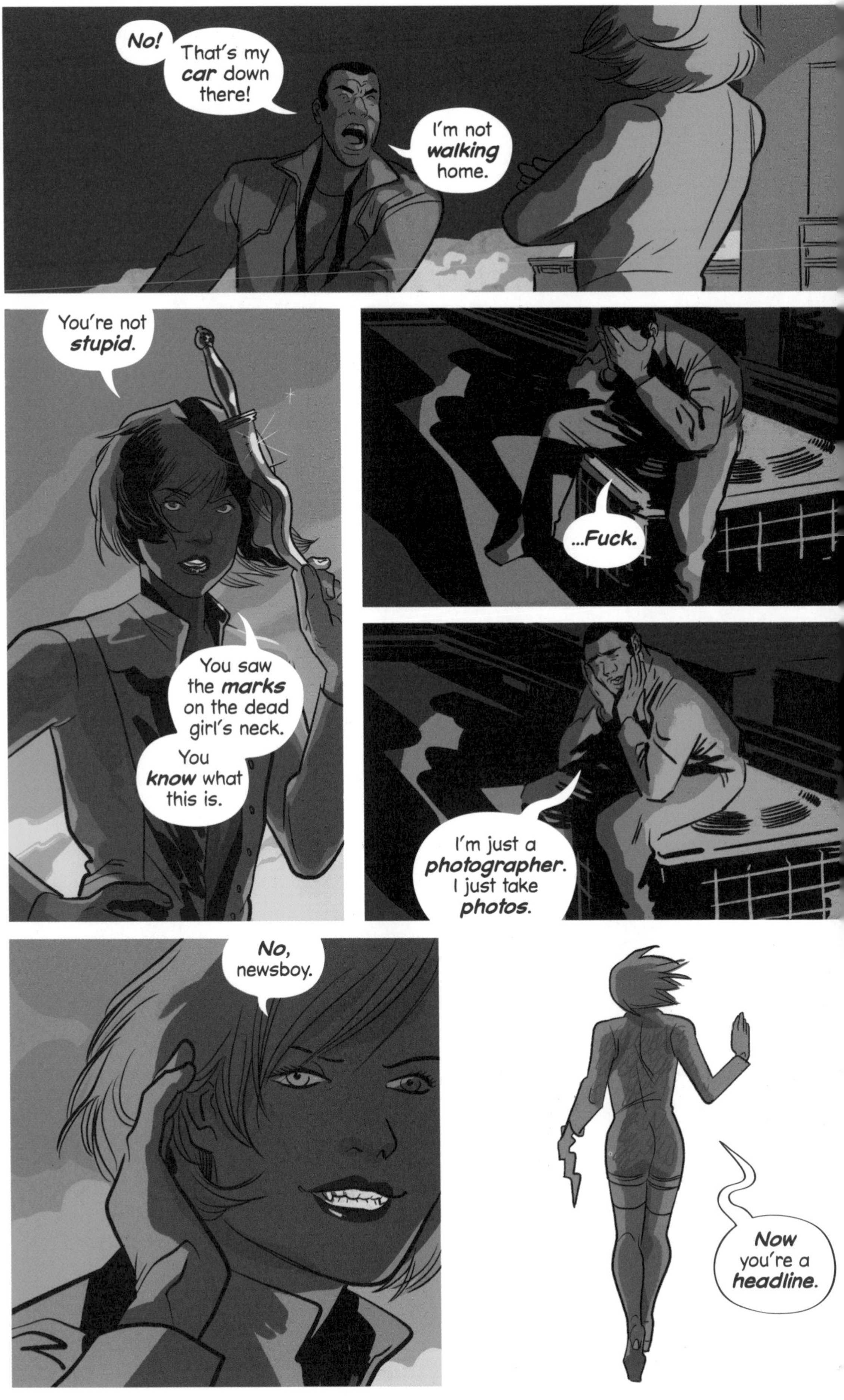
No!
That's my car down there!
I'm not walking home.
You're not stupid.
You saw the marks on the dead girl's neck.
You know what this is.
...Fuck.
I'm just a photographer. I just take photos.
No, newsboy.
Now you're a headline.

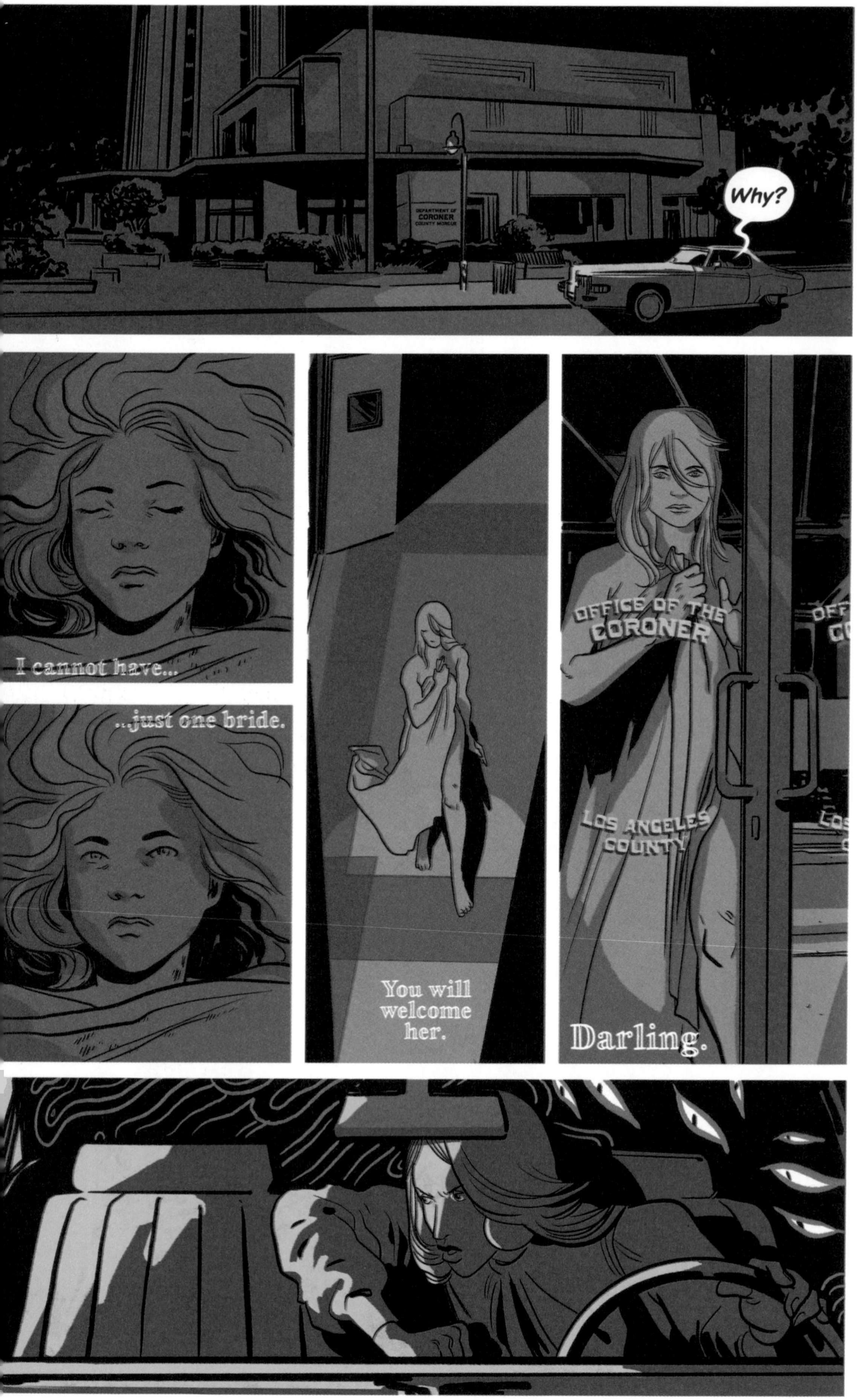
DEPARTMENT OF
CORONER
COUNTY MORGUE
Why?
I cannot have...
...just one bride.
You will welcome her.
OFFICE OF THE
CORONER
LOS ANGELES
COUNTY
Darling.

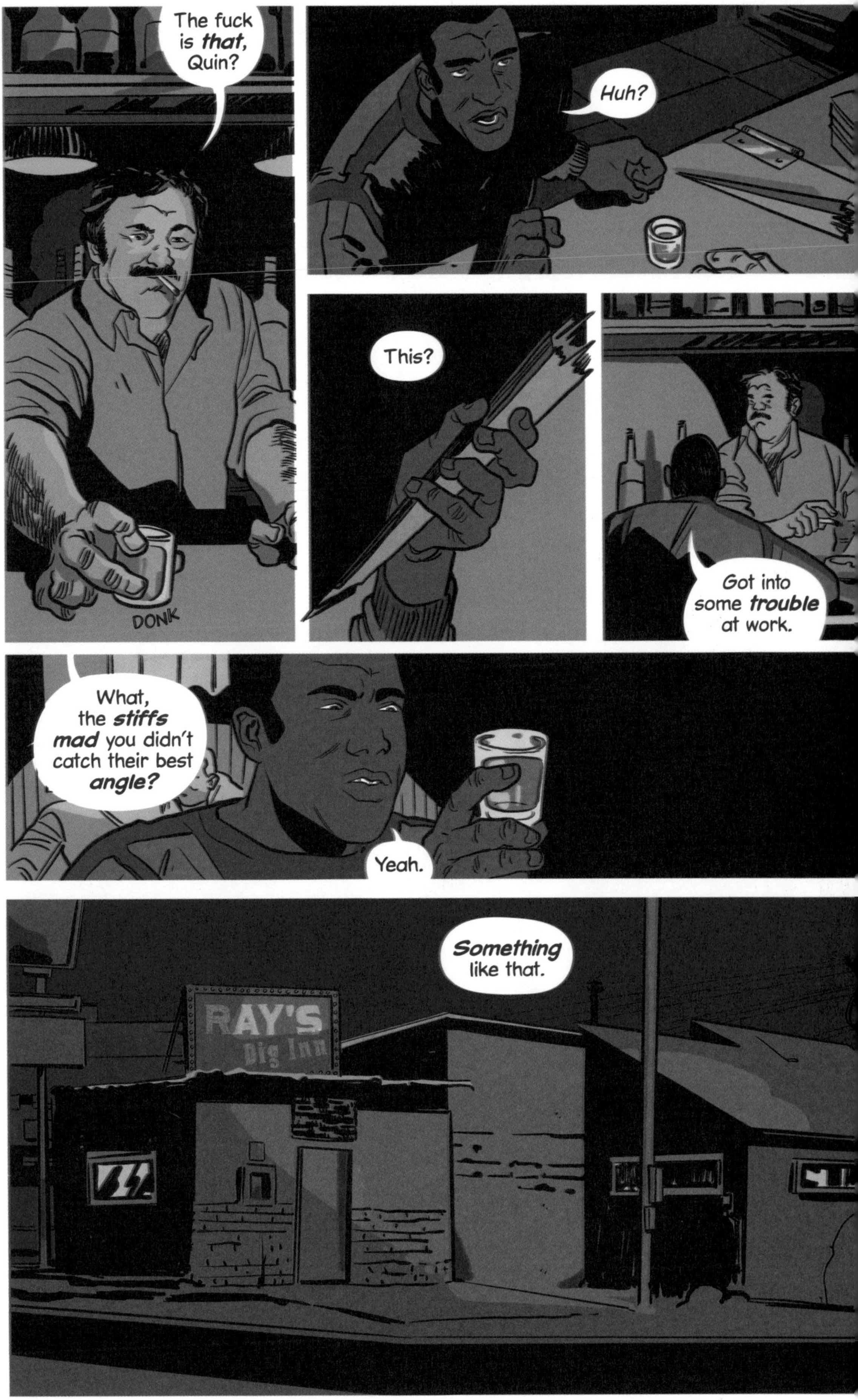

The fuck is *that,* Quin?
DONK
Huh?
This?
Got into some *trouble* at work.
What, the *stiffs mad* you didn't catch their best *angle?*
Yeah.
Something like that.
RAY'S
Big Inn

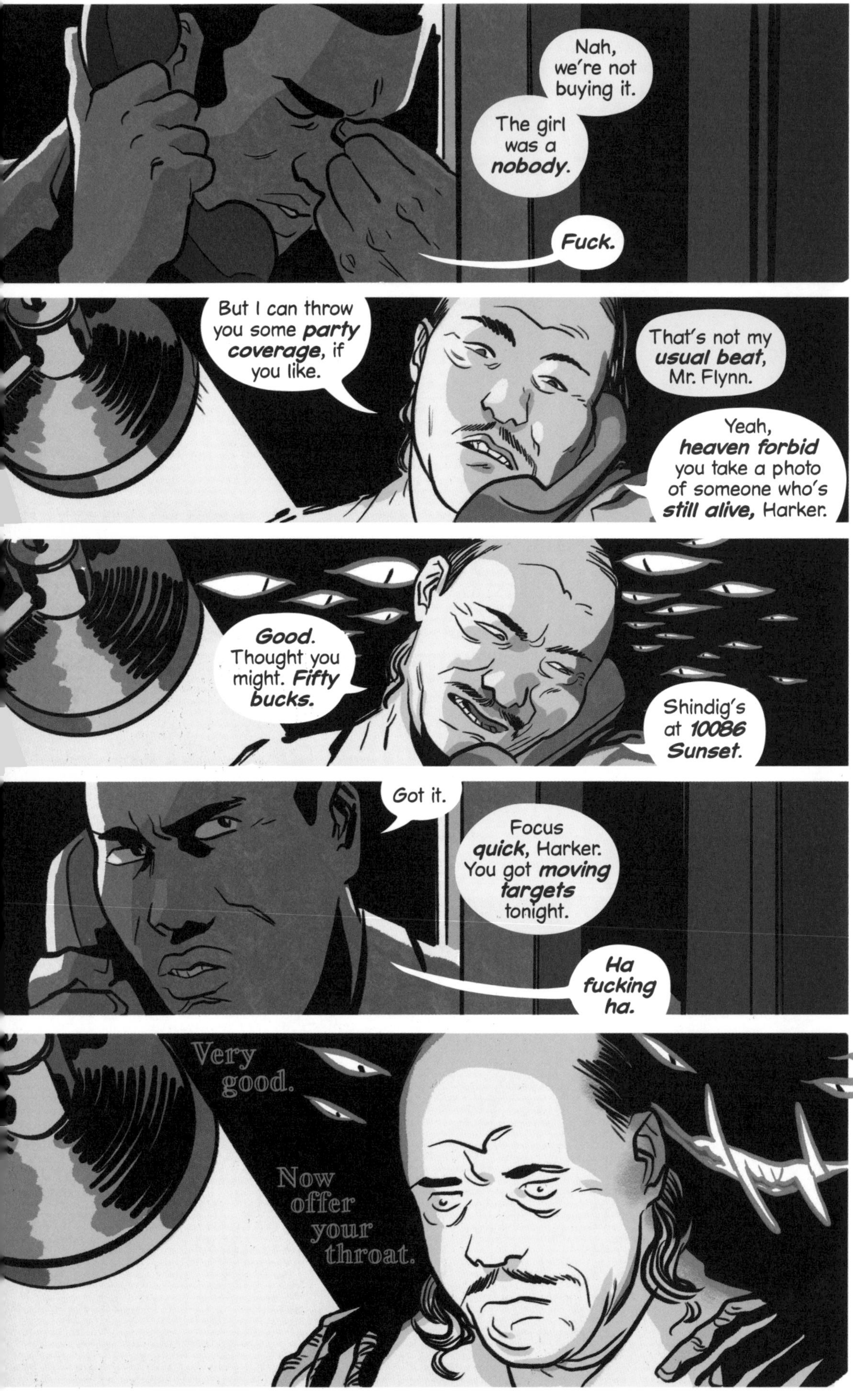
Nah, we're not buying it.
The girl was a **nobody**.
Fuck.
But I can throw you some **party coverage**, if you like.
That's not my **usual beat**, Mr. Flynn.
Yeah, **heaven forbid** you take a photo of someone who's **still alive,** Harker.
Good. Thought you might. **Fifty bucks.**
Shindig's at **10086 Sunset**.
Got it.
Focus **quick,** Harker. You got **moving targets** tonight.
Ha fucking ha.
Very good.
Now offer your throat.

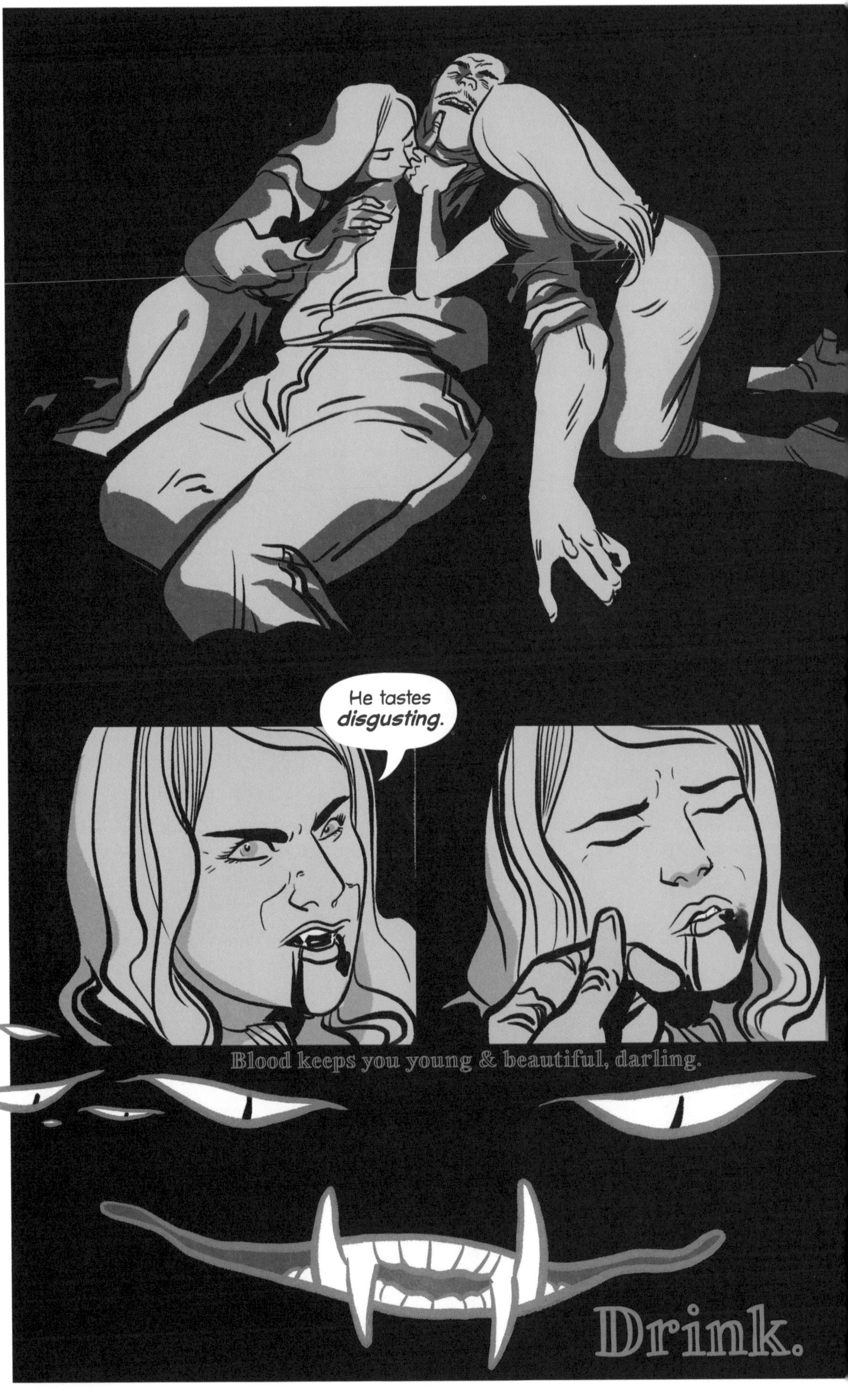
He tastes *disgusting.*
Blood keeps you young & beautiful, darling.
Drink.

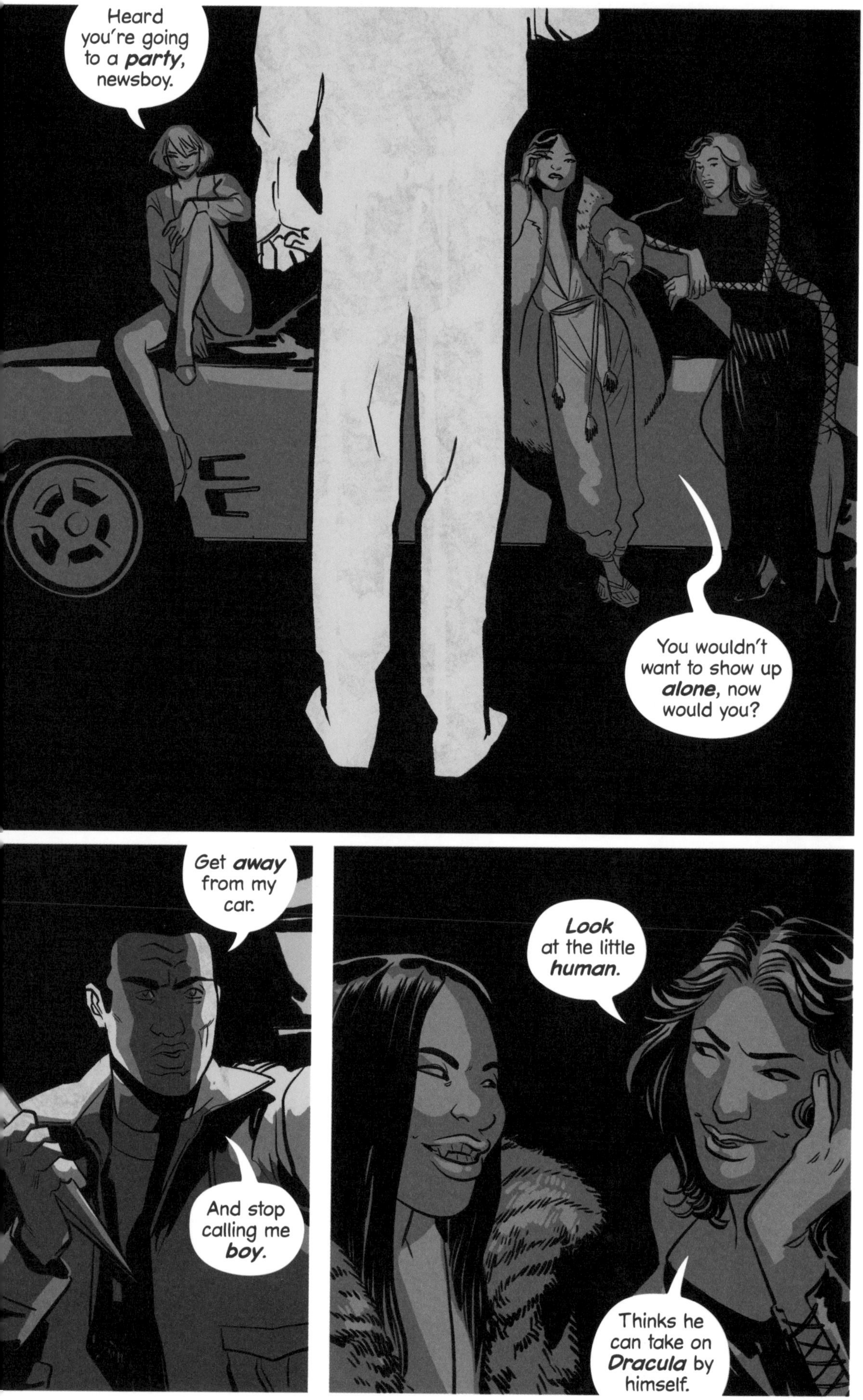
Heard you're going to a *party*, newsboy.
You wouldn't want to show up *alone*, now would you?
Get *away* from my car.
And stop calling me *boy*.
Look at the little *human*.
Thinks he can take on *Dracula* by himself.

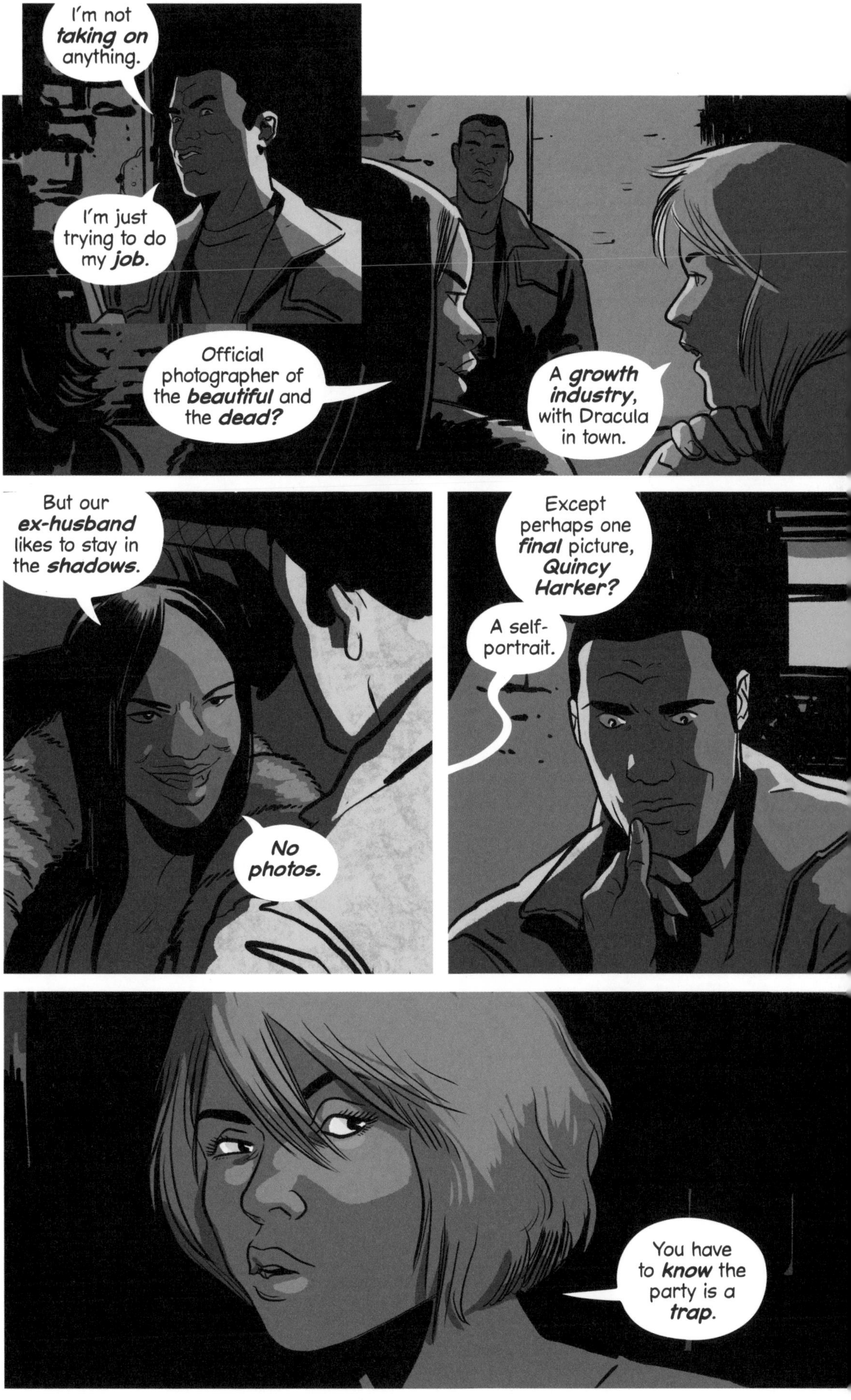
I'm not ***taking on*** anything.
I'm just trying to do my ***job.***
Official photographer of the ***beautiful*** and the ***dead?***
A ***growth industry***, with Dracula in town.
But our ***ex-husband*** likes to stay in the ***shadows.***
No photos.
Except perhaps one ***final*** picture, ***Quincy Harker?***
A self-portrait.
You have to ***know*** the party is a ***trap.***

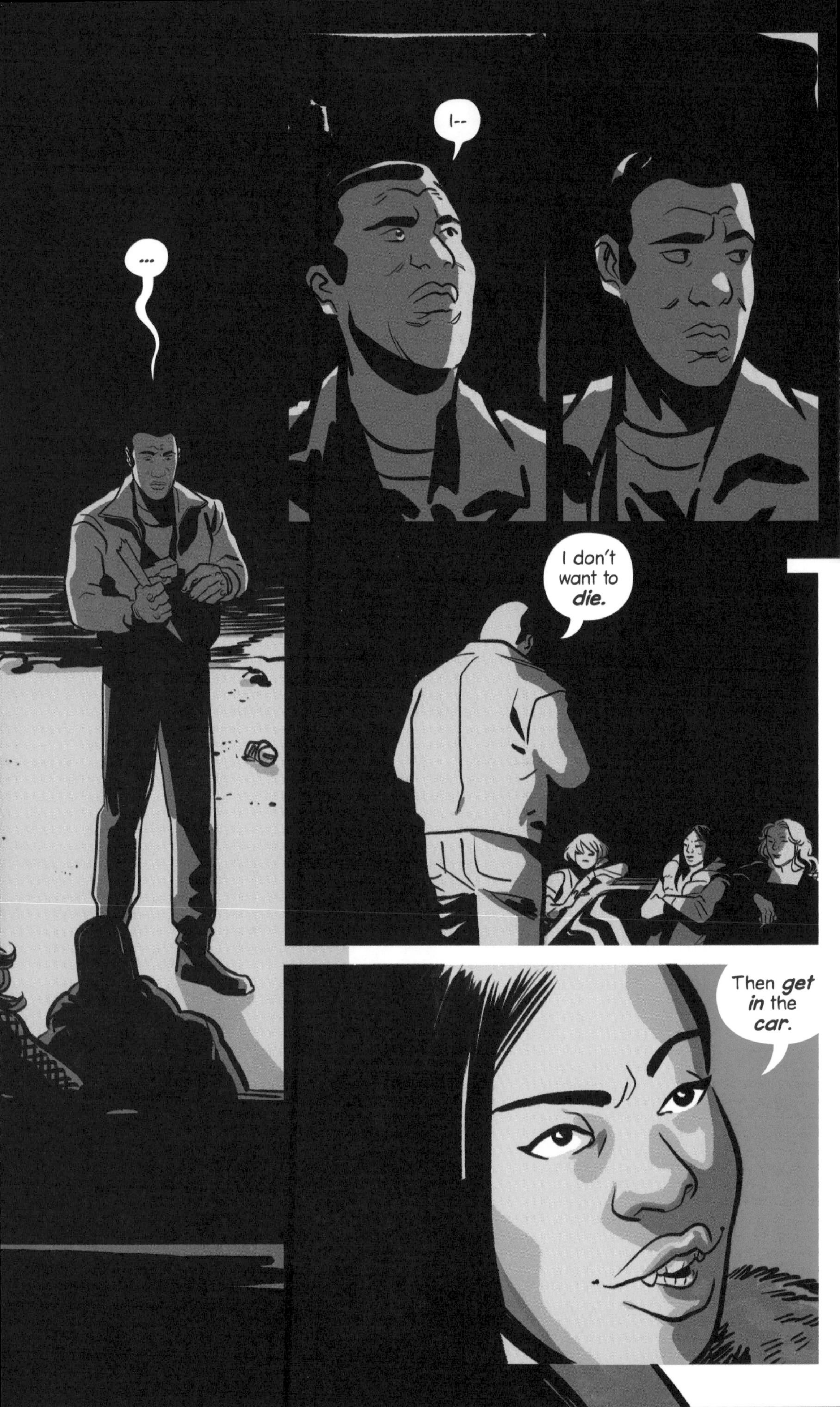
...
I--
I don't want to die.
Then get in the car.

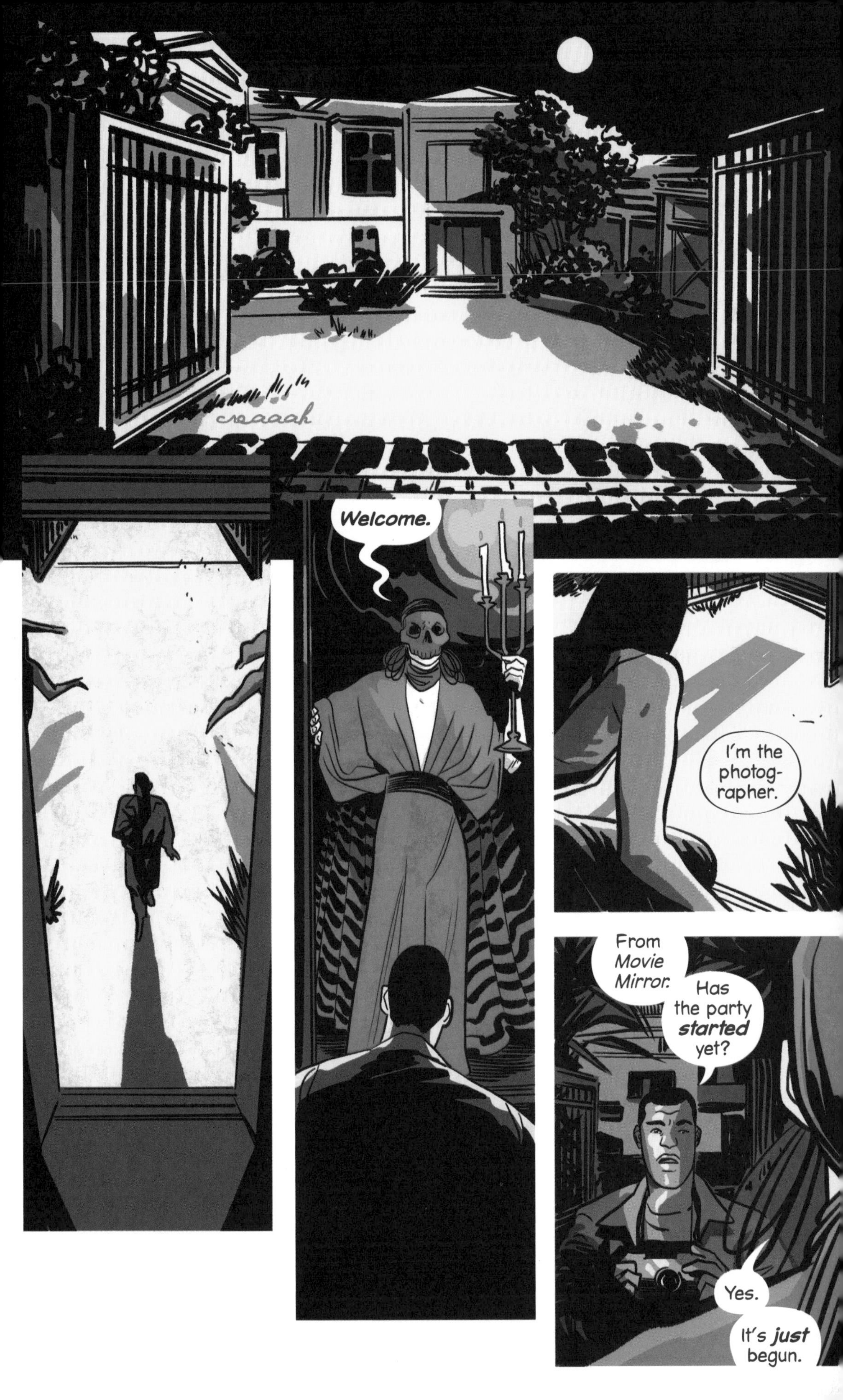
creaaah
Welcome.
I'm the photographer.
From Movie Mirror.
Has the party *started* yet?
Yes.
It's *just* begun.

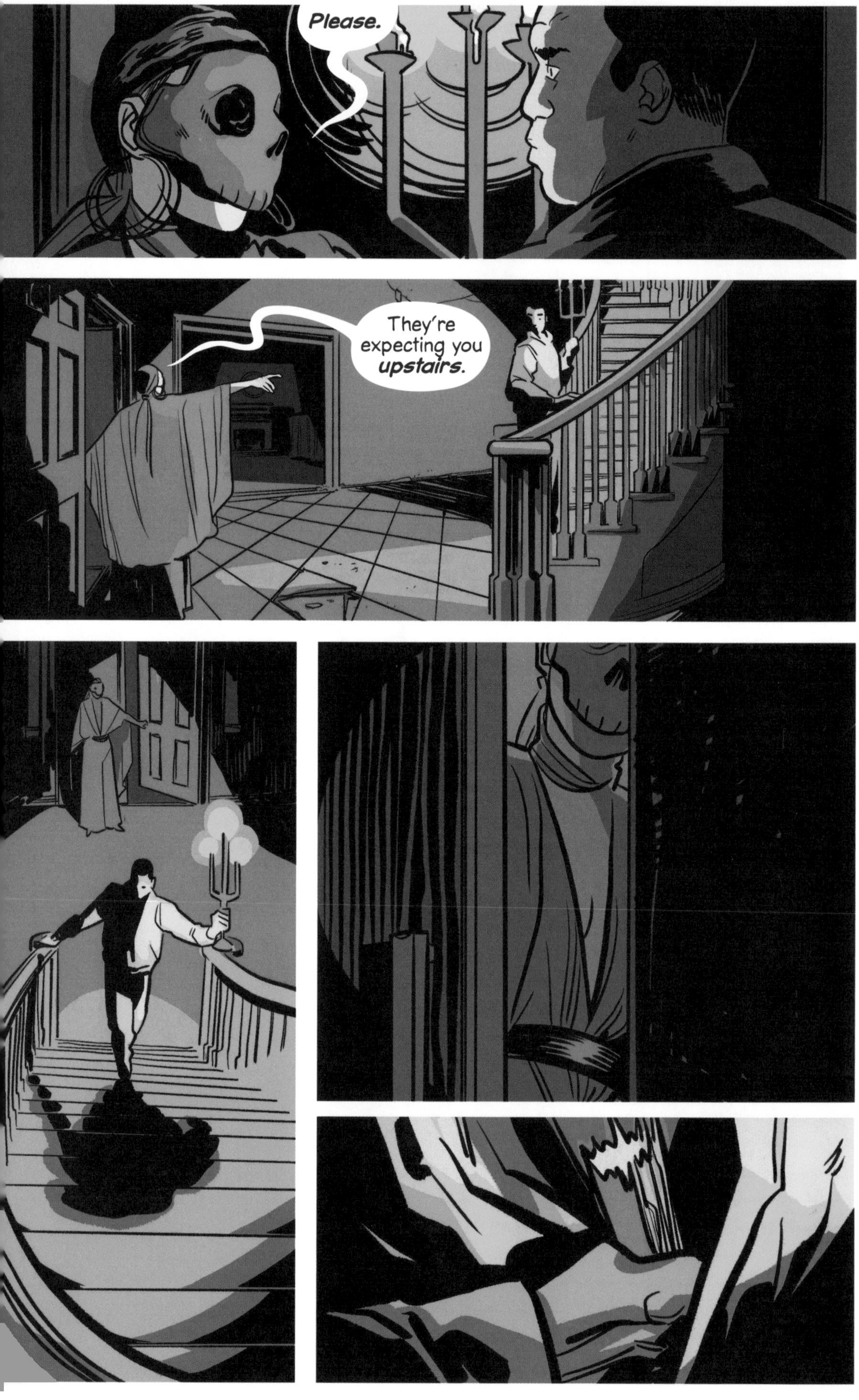
Please.
They're expecting you *upstairs.*

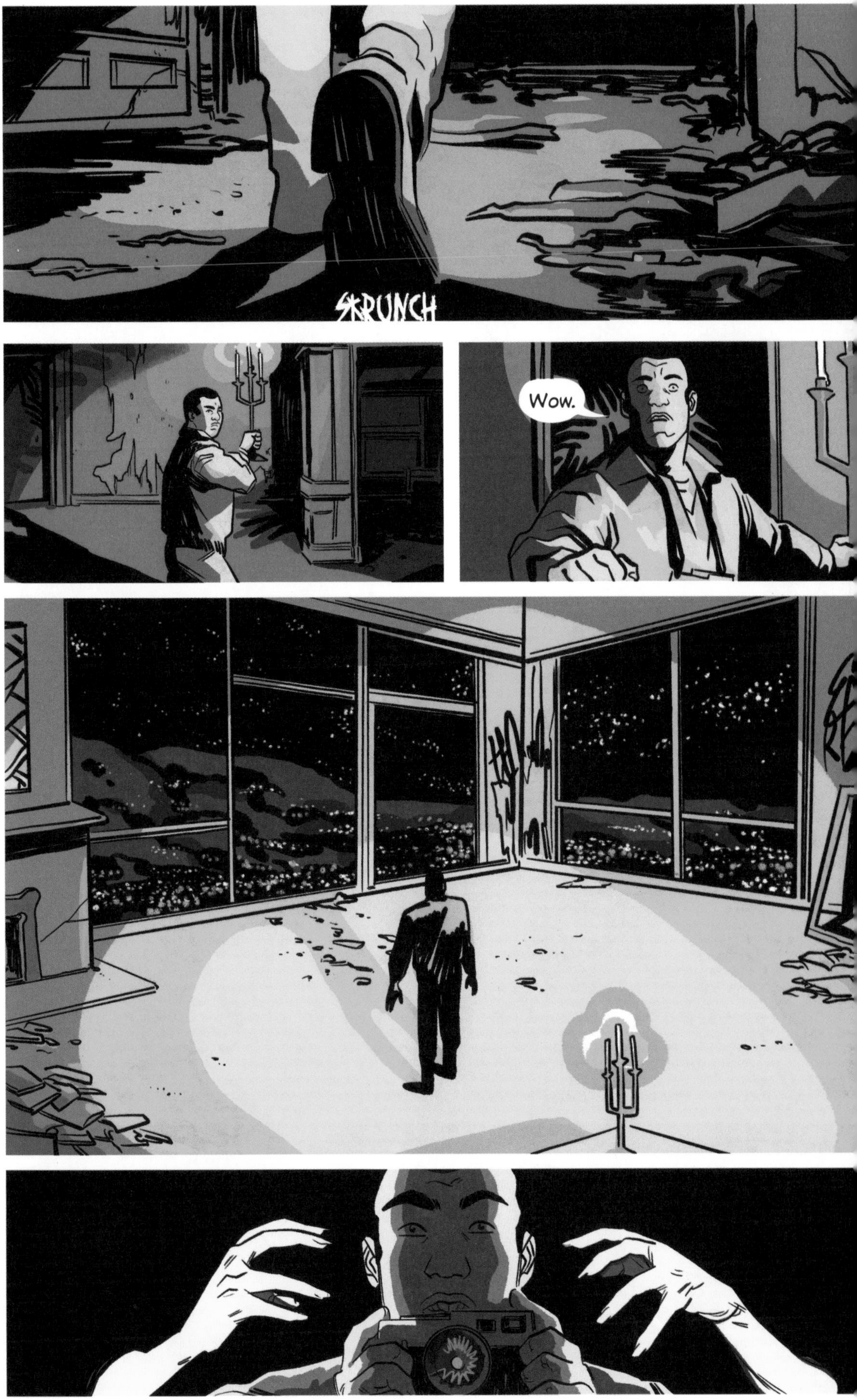
SKRUNCH
Wow.

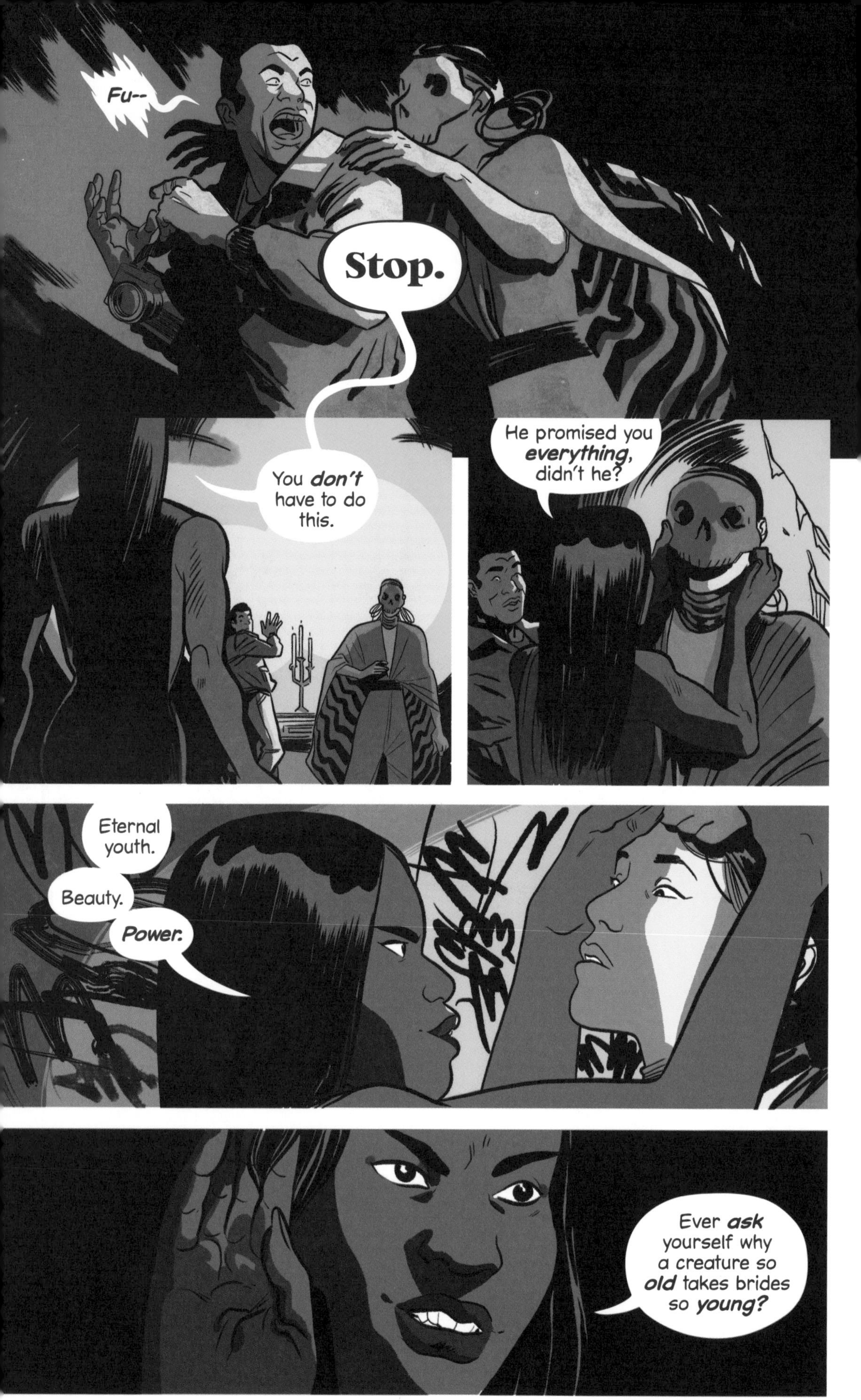
Fu--
Stop.
You *don't* have to do this.
He promised you *everything,* didn't he?
Eternal youth.
Beauty.
Power.
Ever *ask* yourself why a creature so *old* takes brides so *young?*

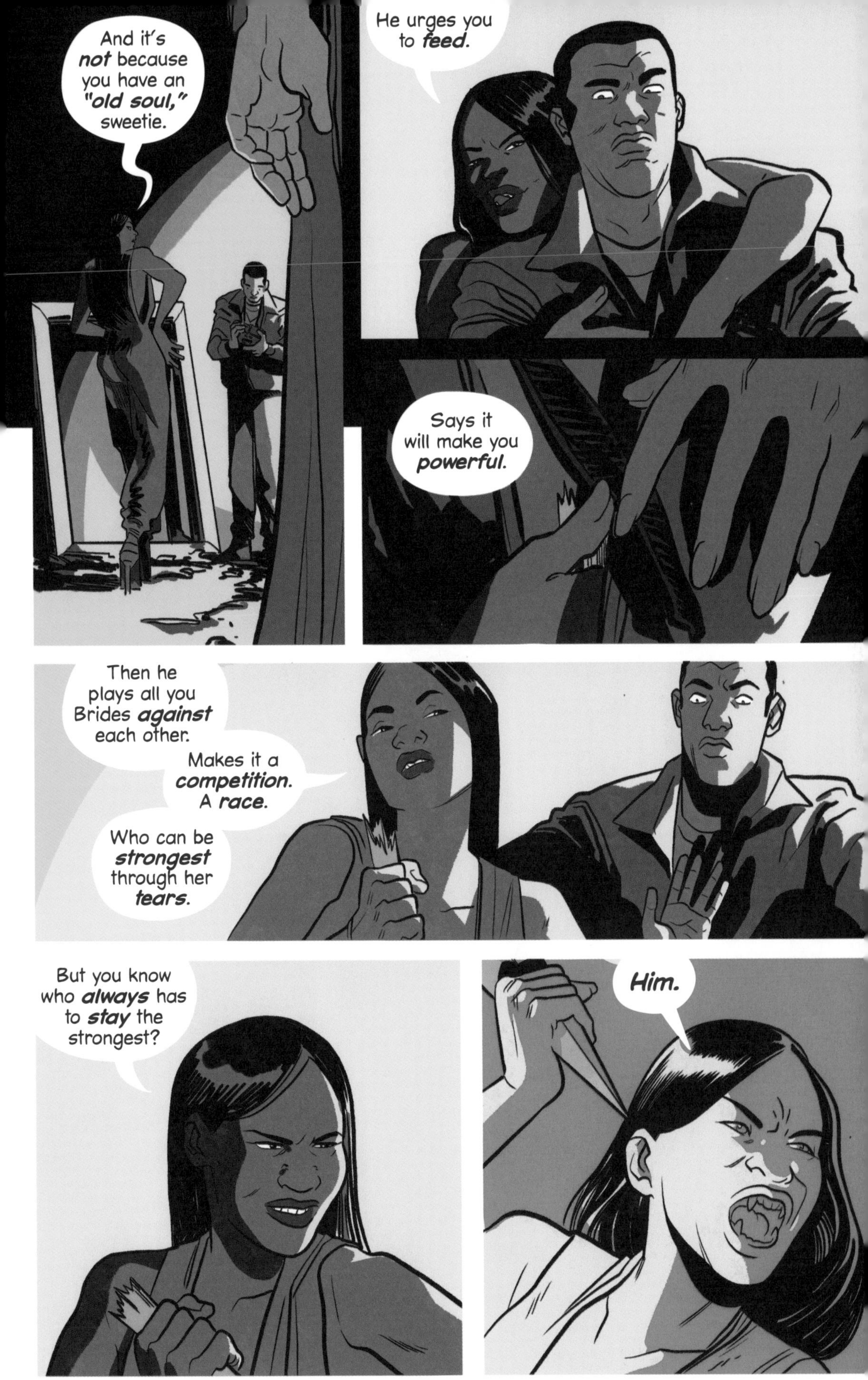

And it's *not* because you have an *"old soul,"* sweetie.
He urges you to *feed*.
Says it will make you *powerful*.
Then he plays all you Brides *against* each other.
Makes it a *competition*. A *race*.
Who can be *strongest* through her *tears*.
But you know who *always* has to *stay* the strongest?
Him.

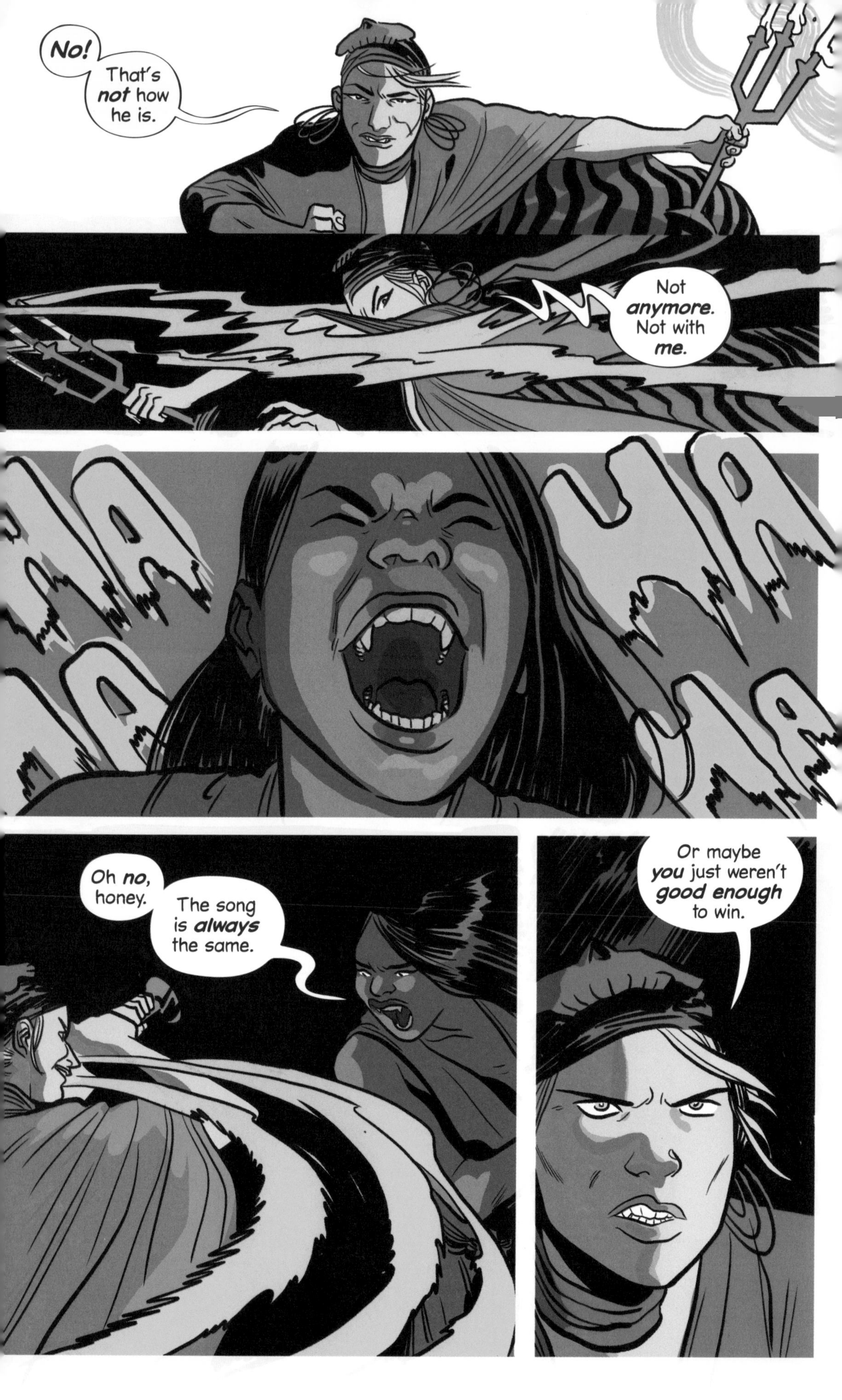
No!
That's not how he is.
Not anymore. Not with me.
HA HA
HA HA
Oh no, honey.
The song is always the same.
Or maybe you just weren't good enough to win.

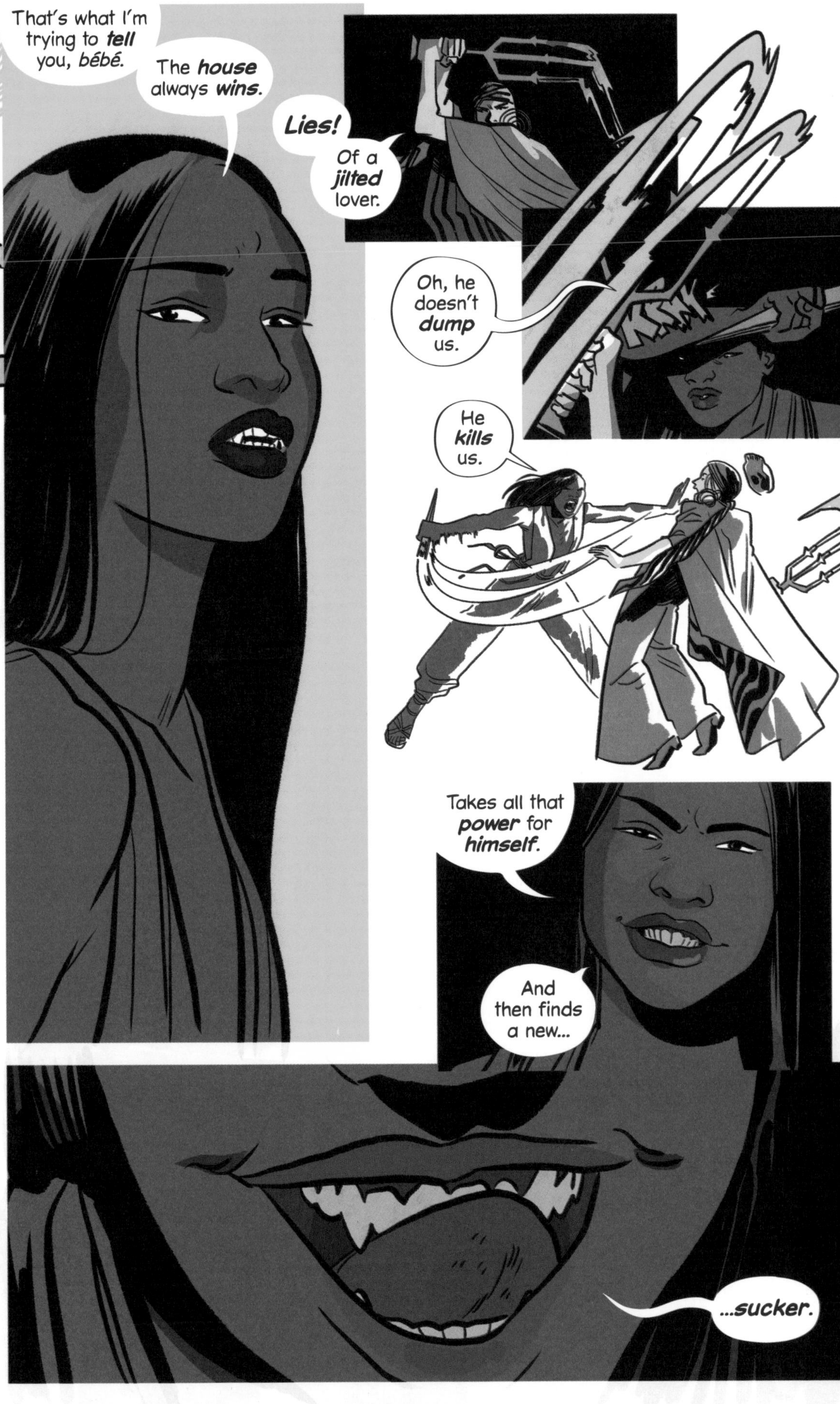

That's what I'm trying to **tell** you, *bébé.*
The **house** always **wins.**
Lies!
Of a **jilted** lover.
Oh, he doesn't **dump** us.
He **kills** us.
Takes all that **power** for **himself**.
And then finds a new...
...sucker.

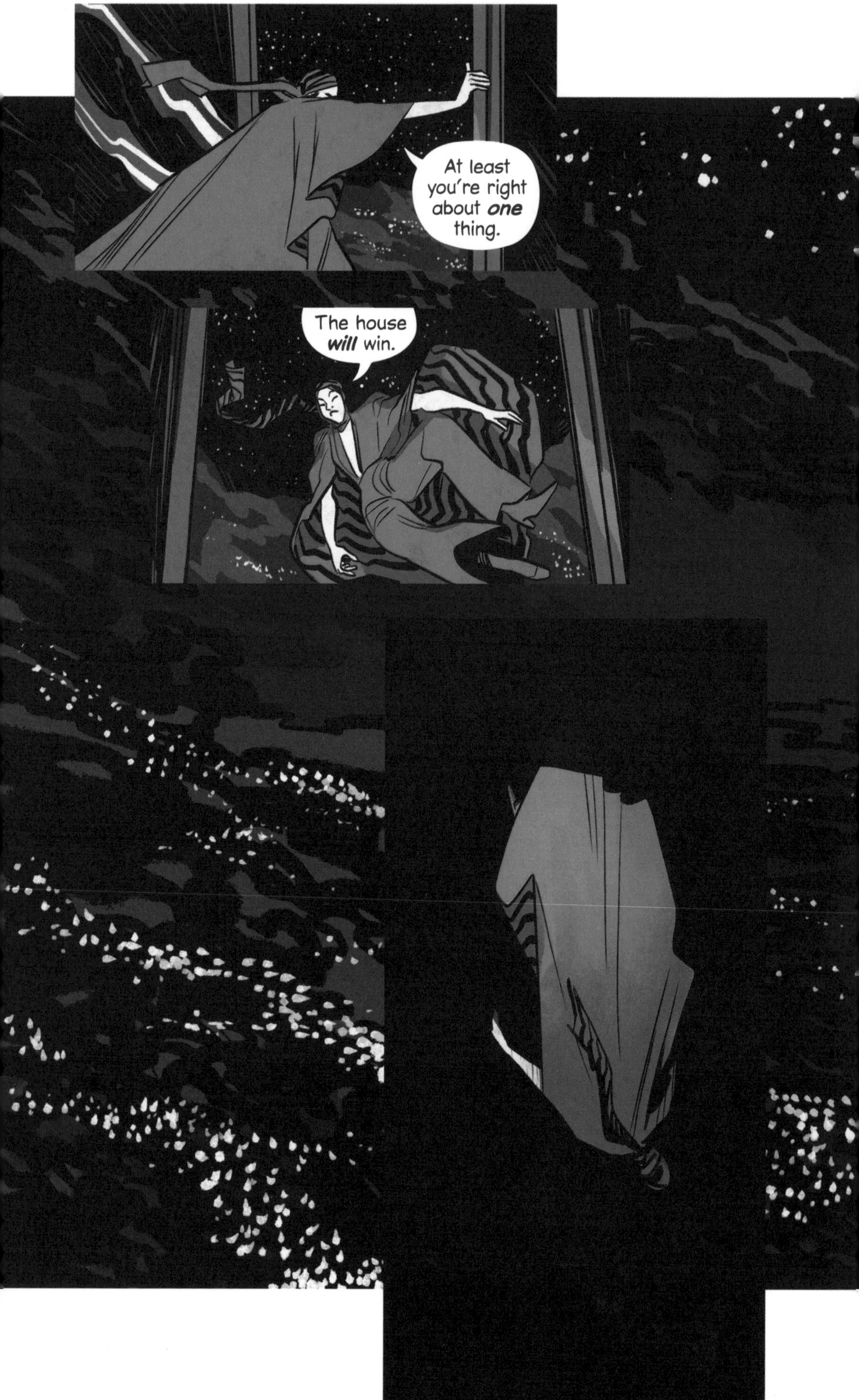
At least you're right about *one* thing.
The house *will* win.

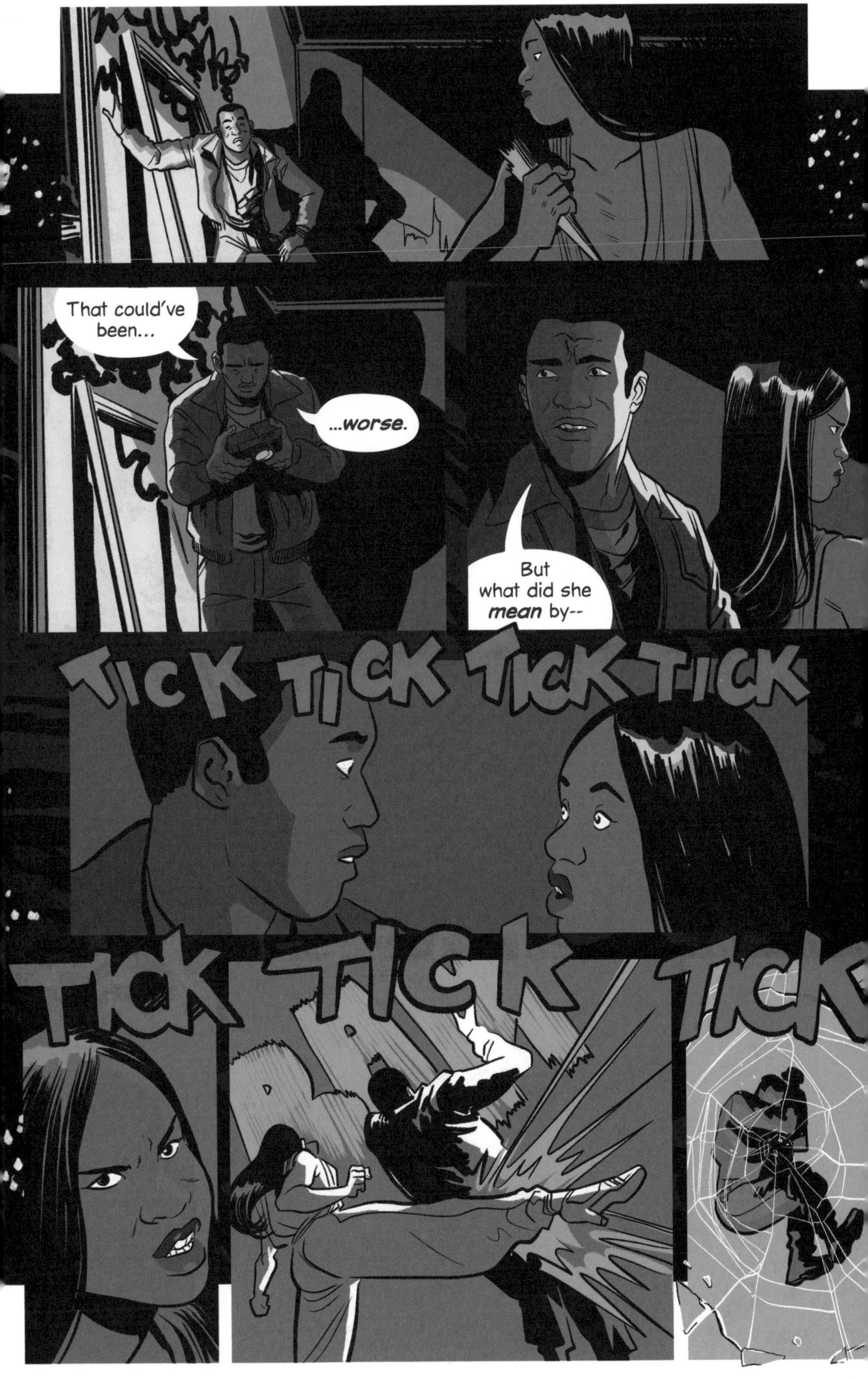
That could've been...
...worse.
But what did she *mean* by--
TICK TICK TICK TICK
TICK TICK TICK

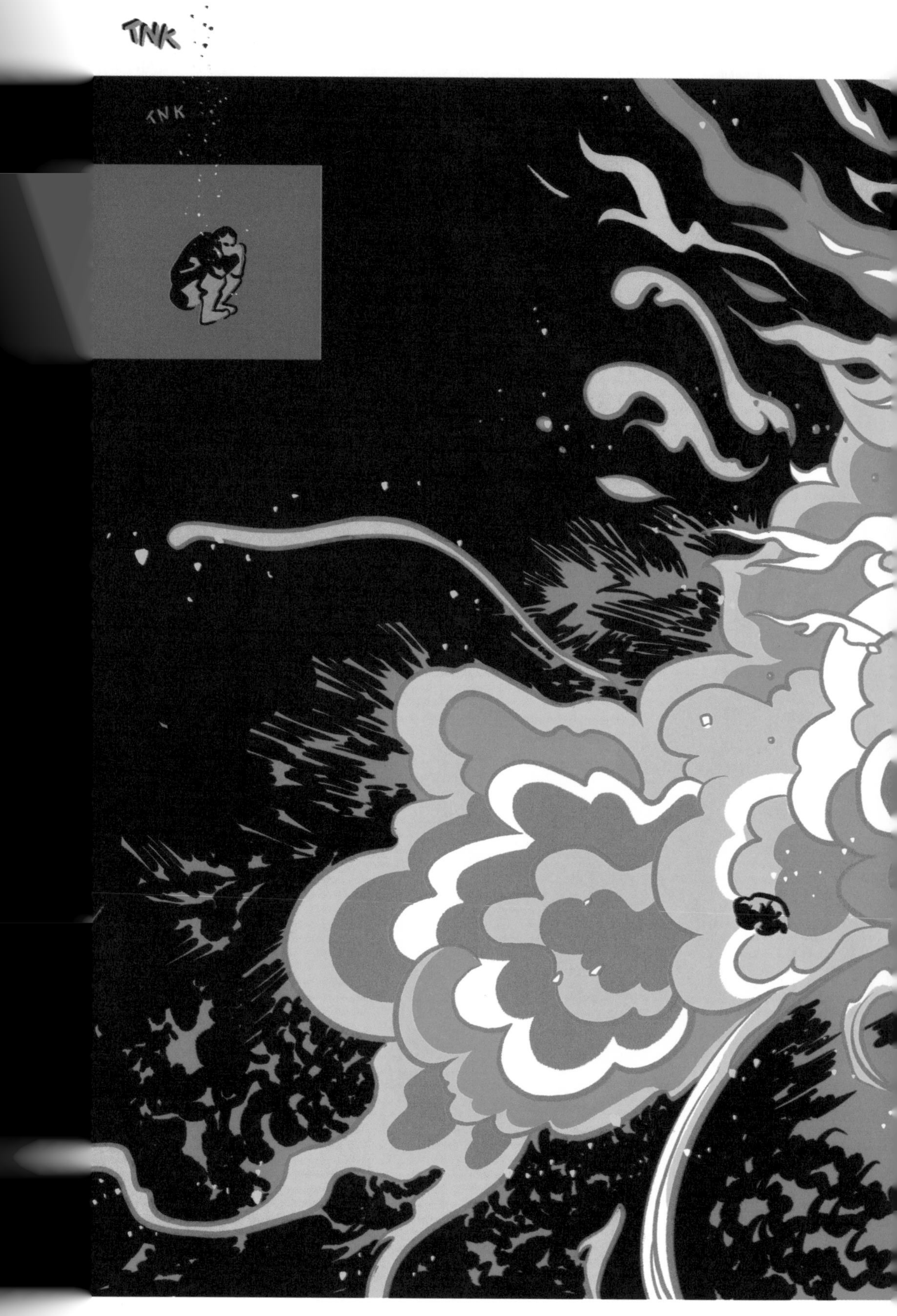
TNK
TNK

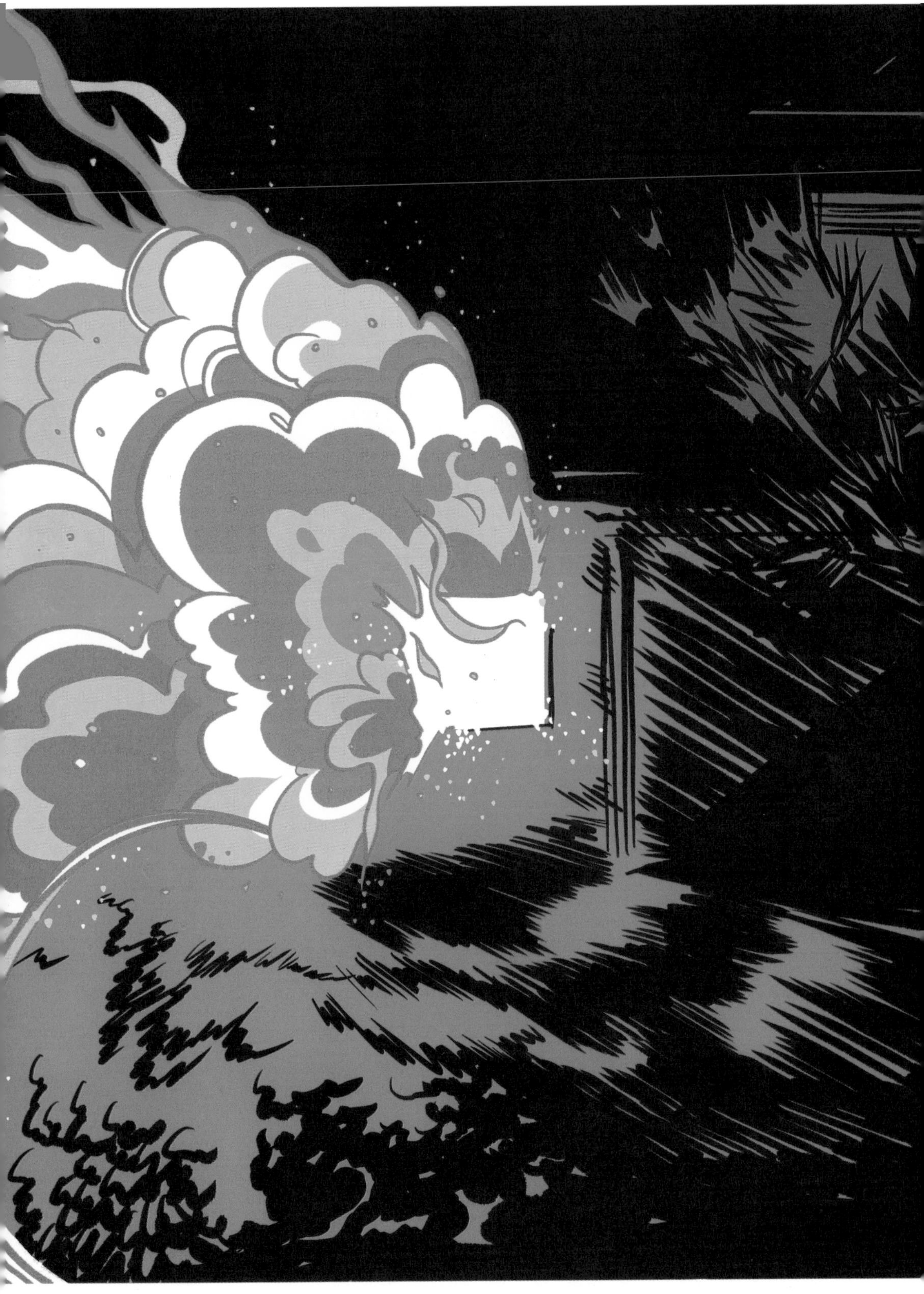

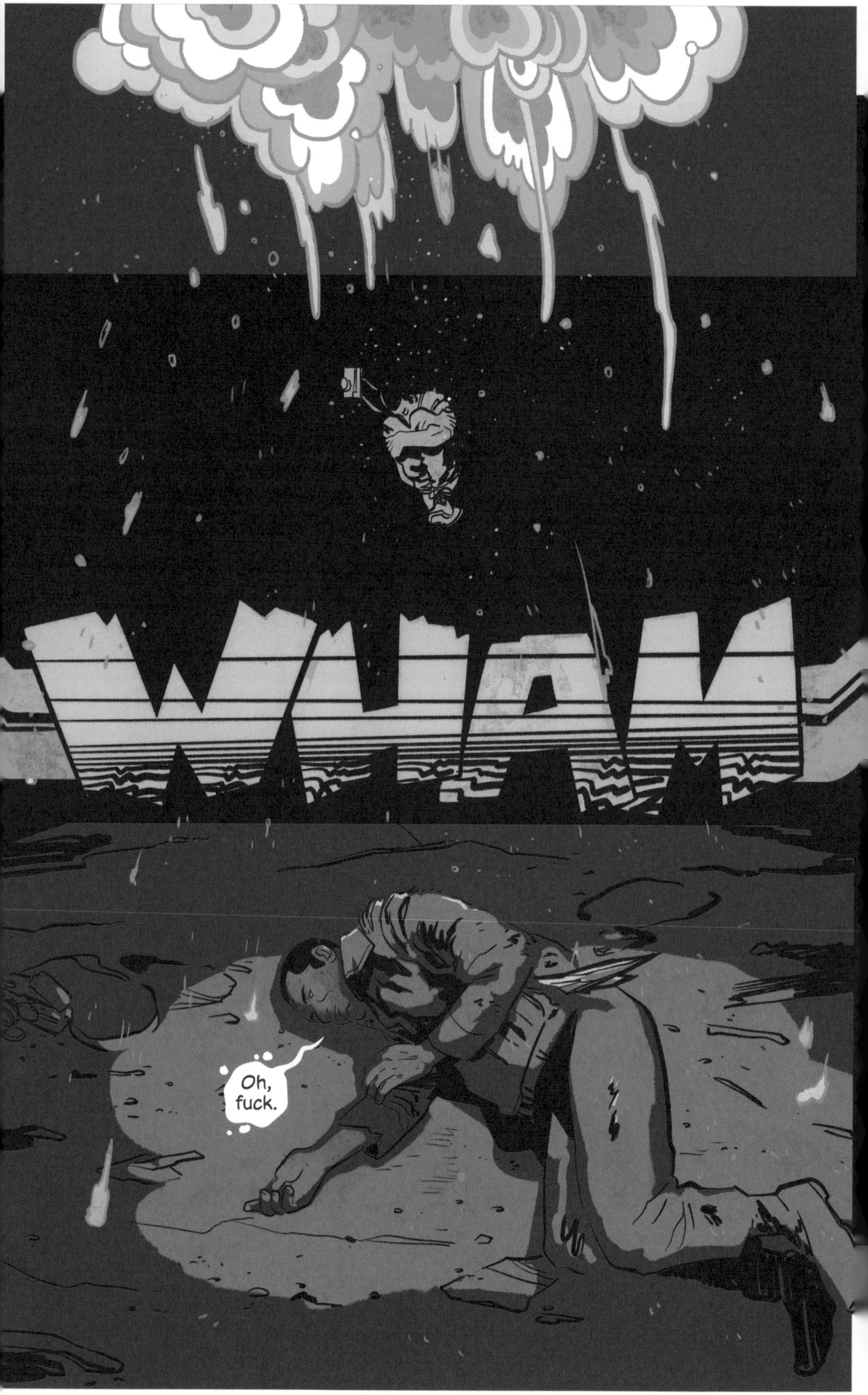
WHAM
Oh, fuck.

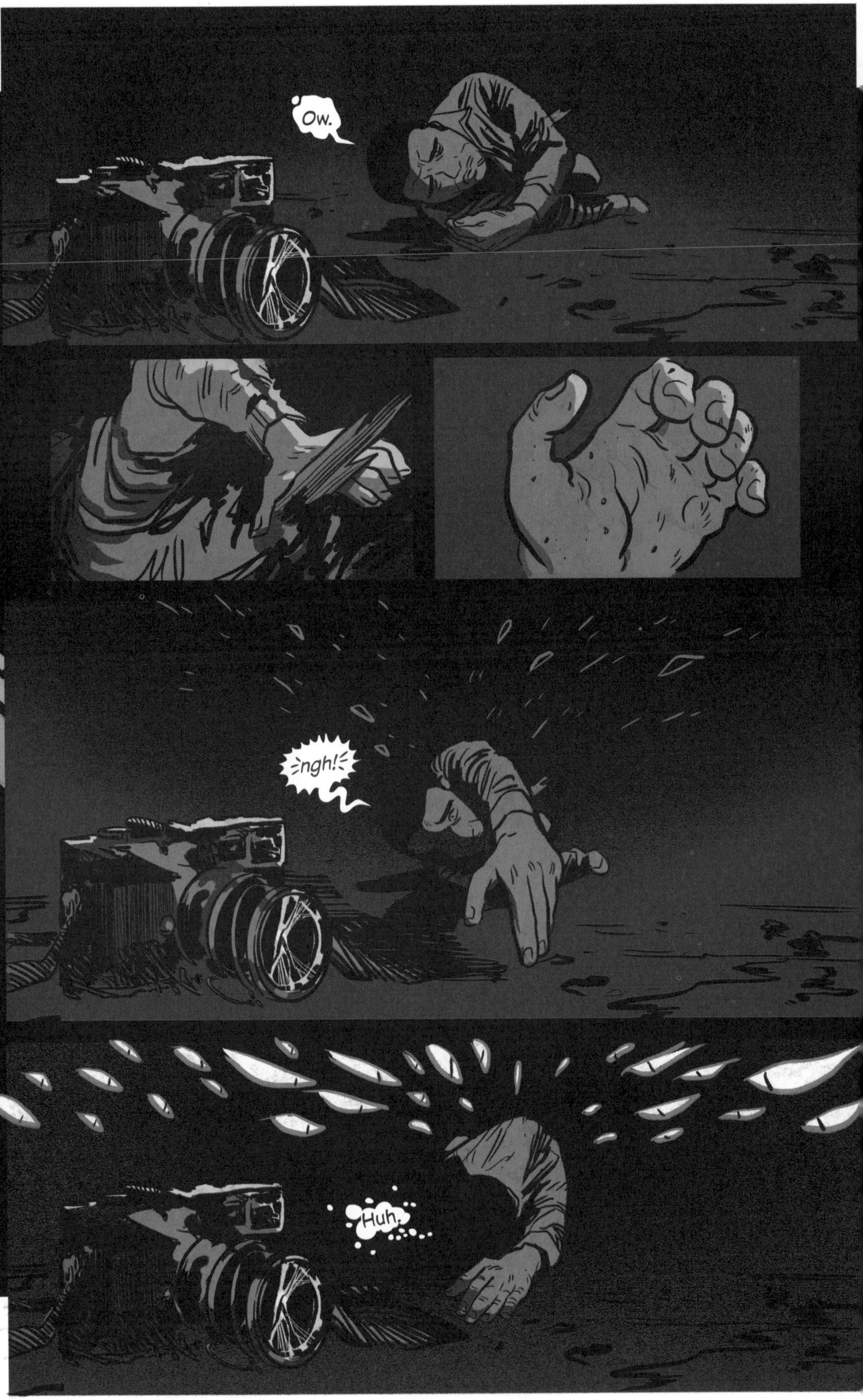
Ow.
ngh!
Huh.

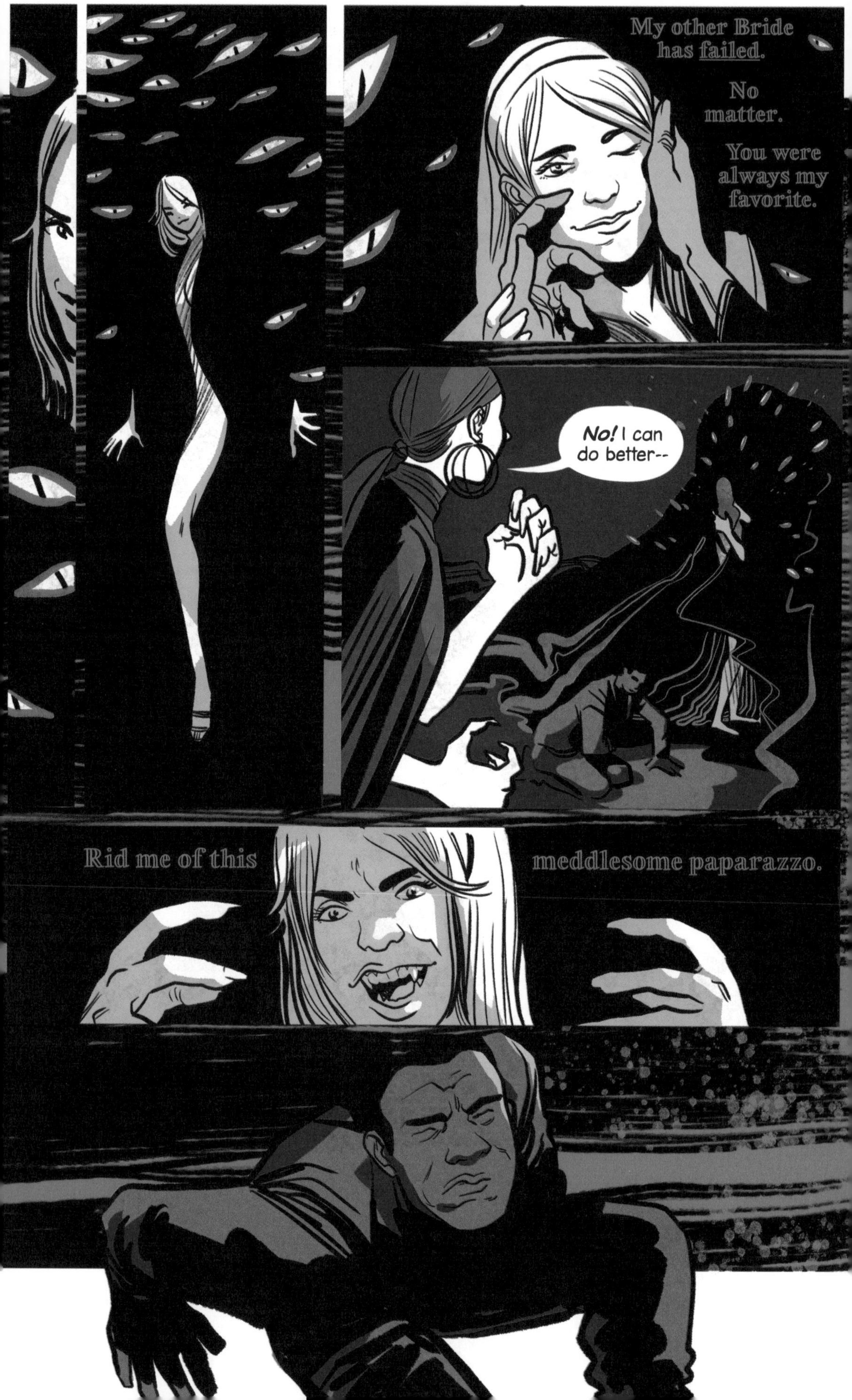

My other Bride has failed.
No matter.
You were always my favorite.
No! I can do better--
Rid me of this
meddlesome paparazzo.

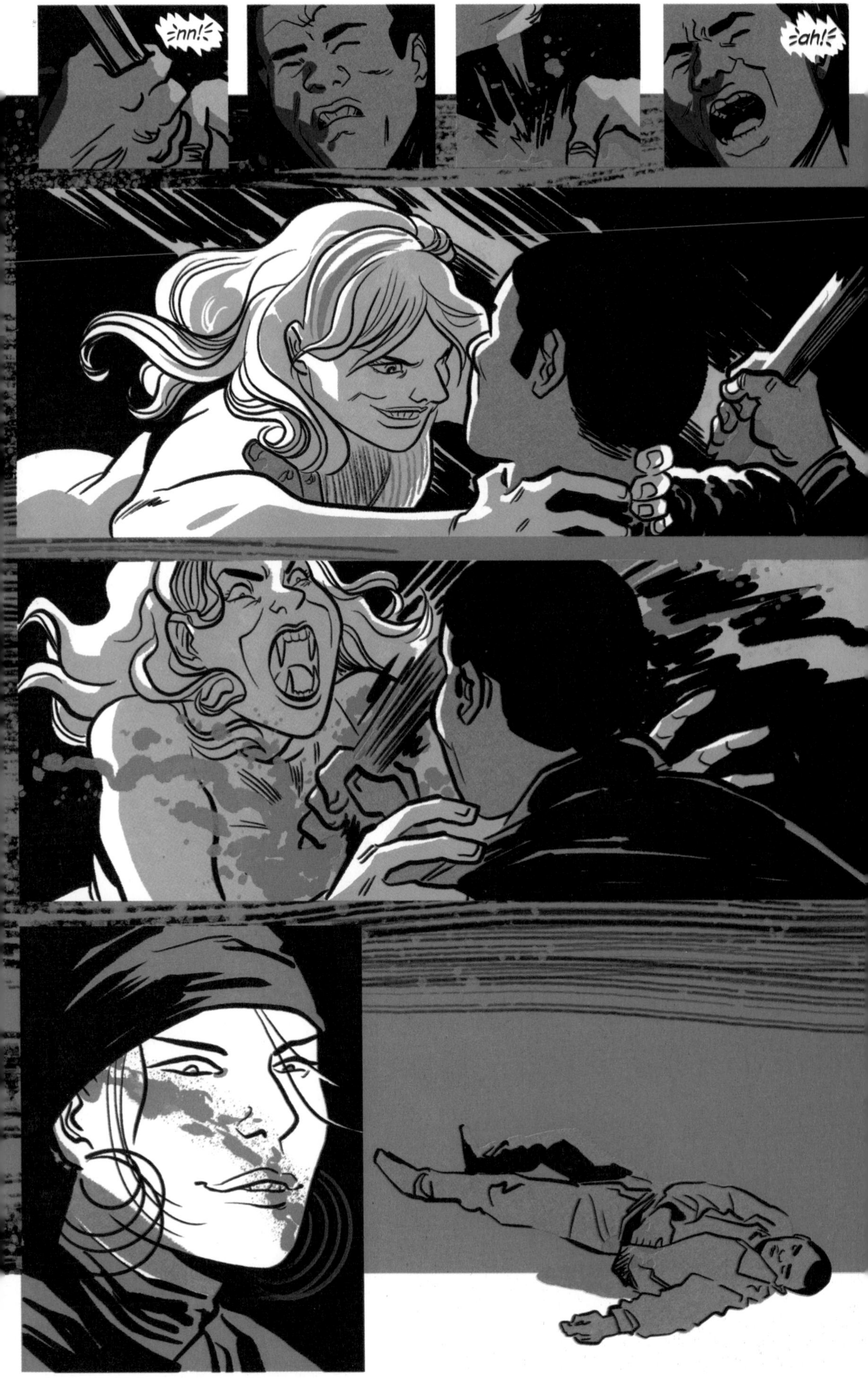
nn!
ah!

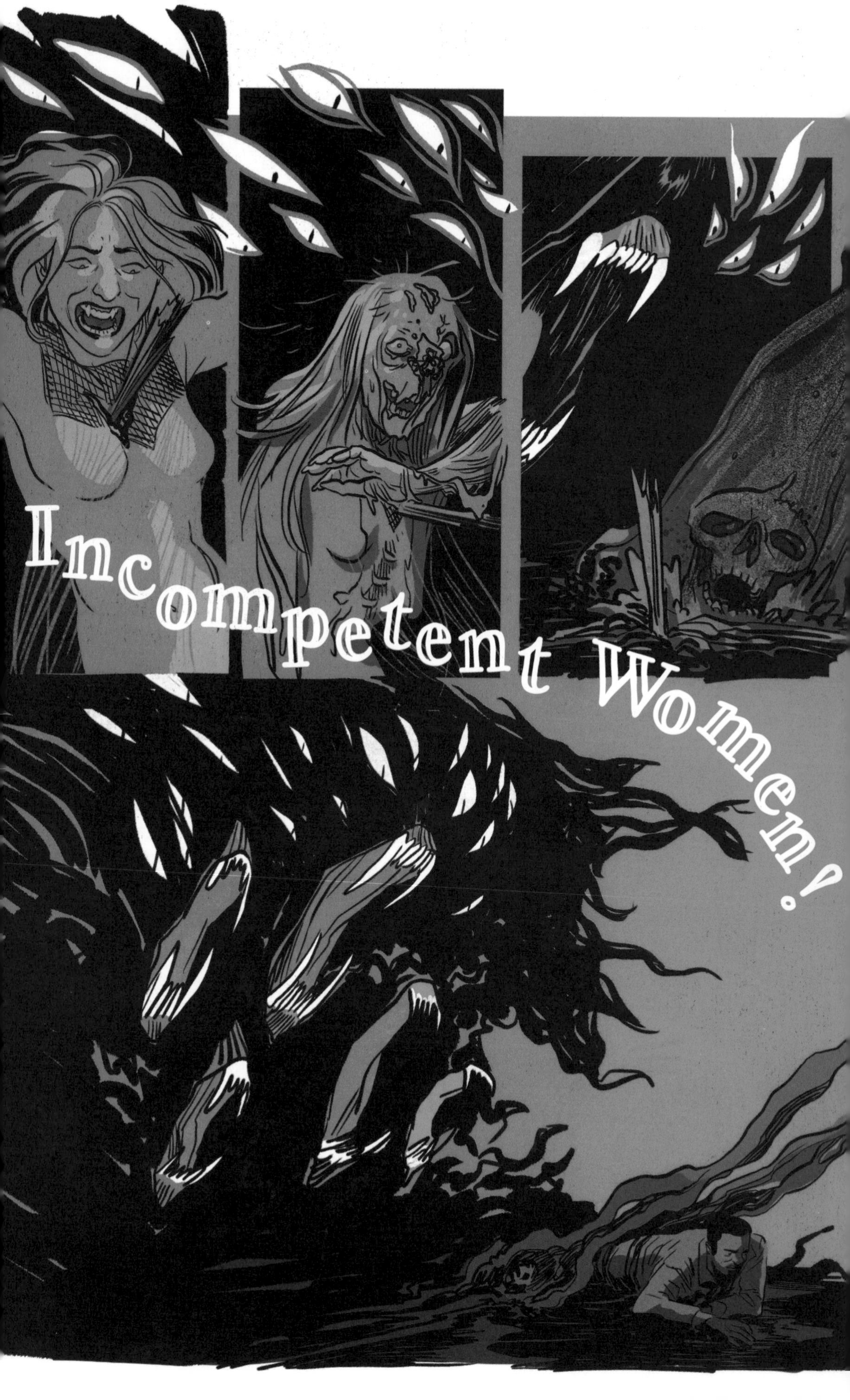
Incompetent Women!

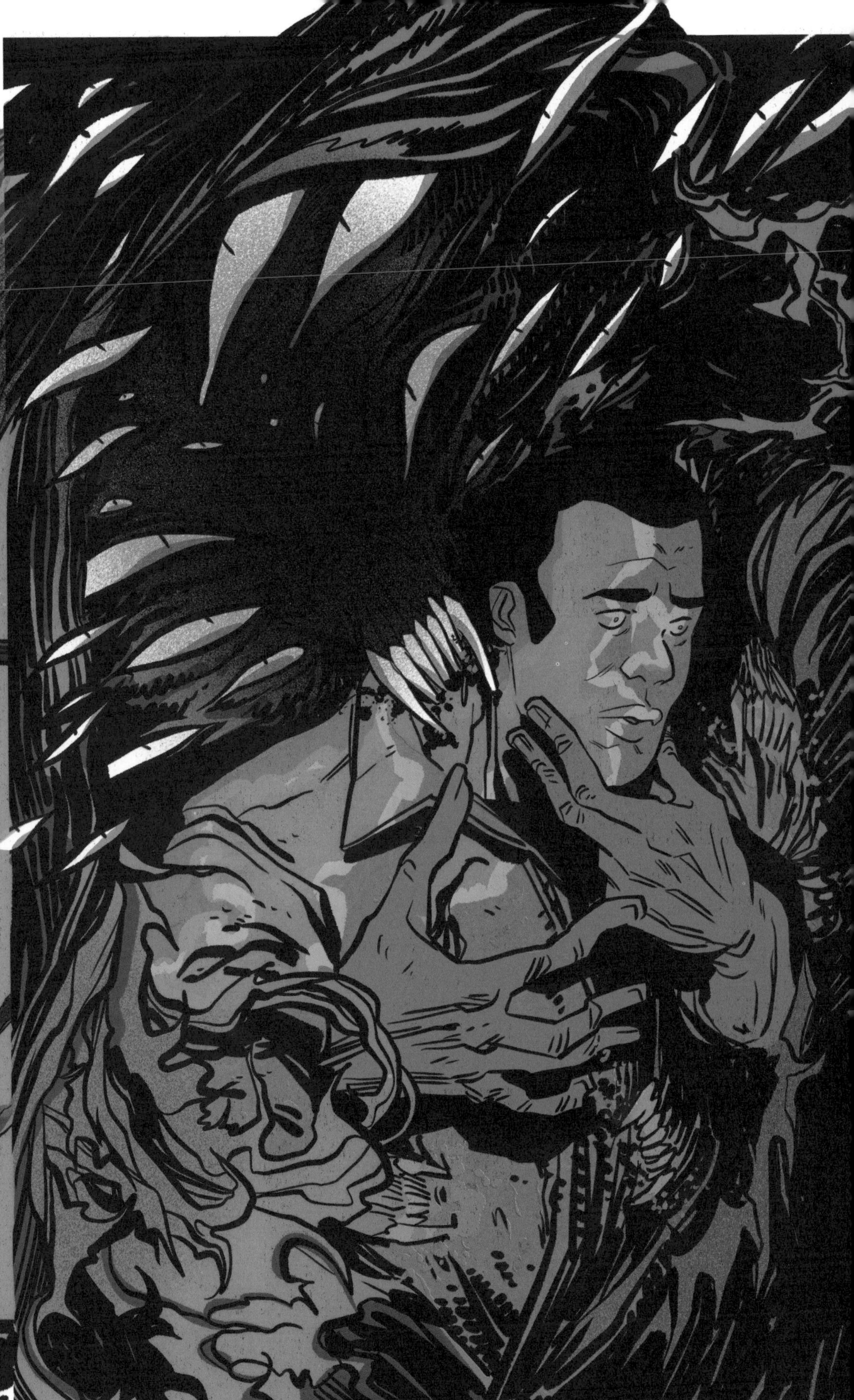

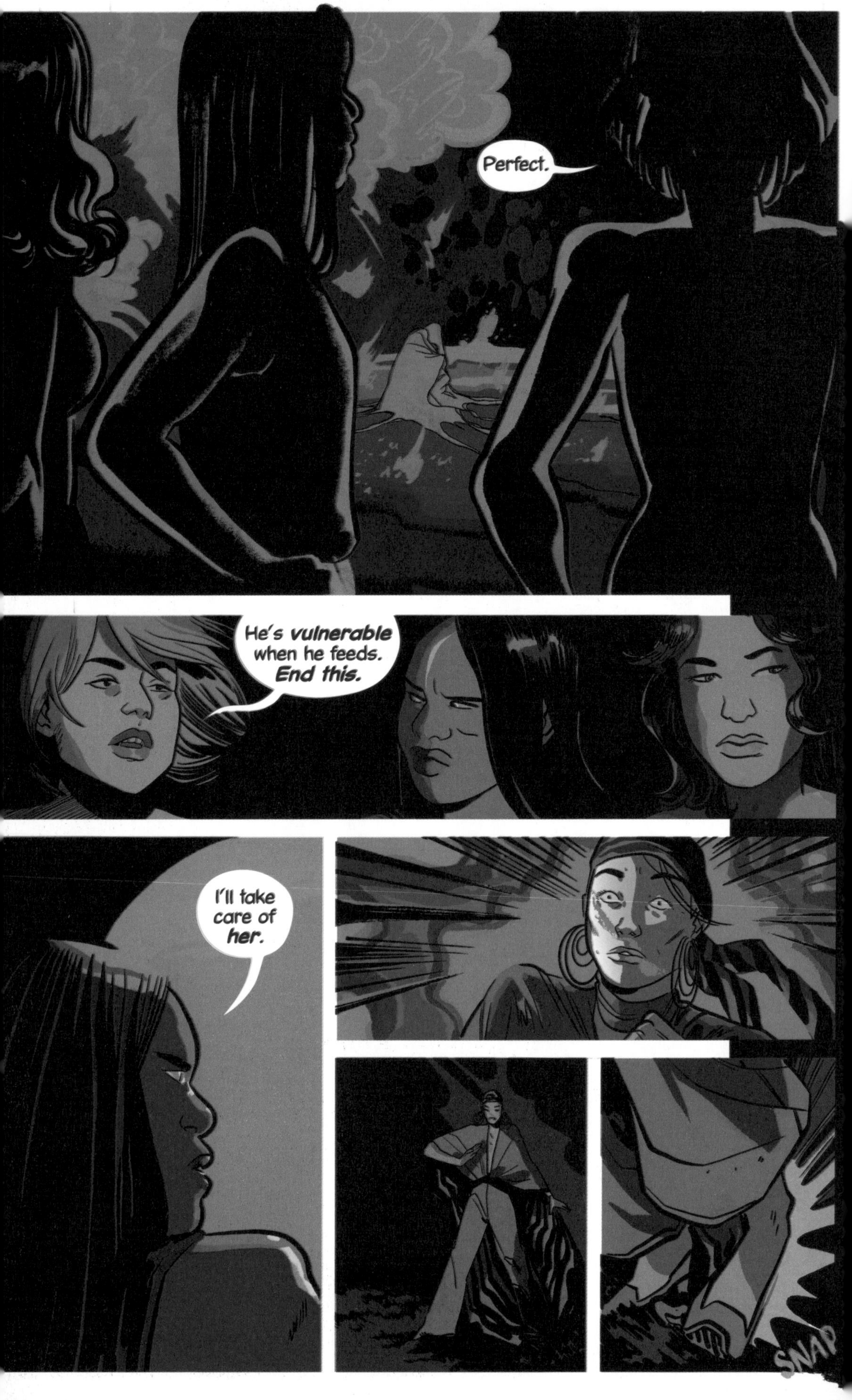
Perfect.
He's *vulnerable* when he feeds. *End this.*
I'll take care of *her.*
SNAP

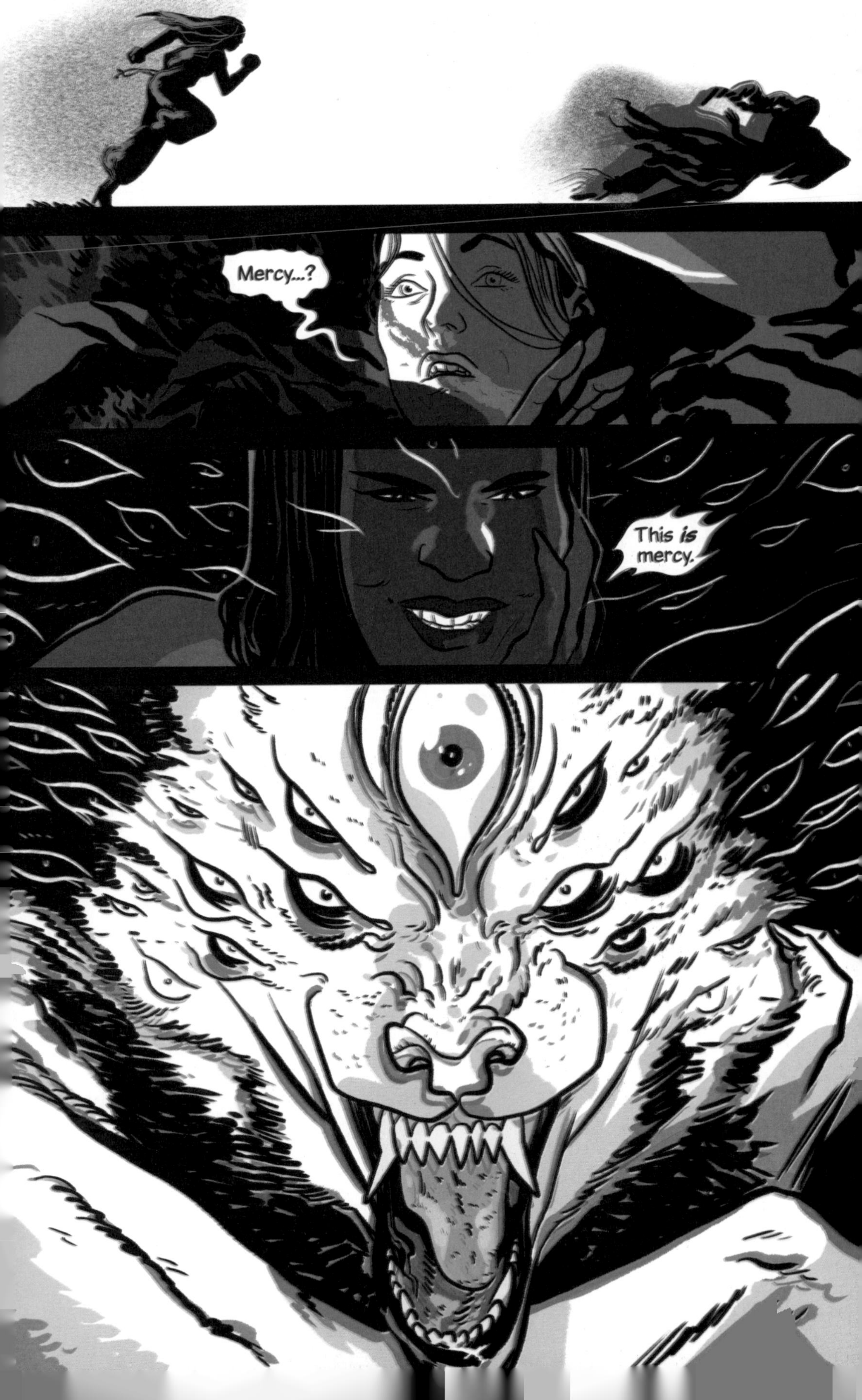
Mercy...?
This *is* mercy.

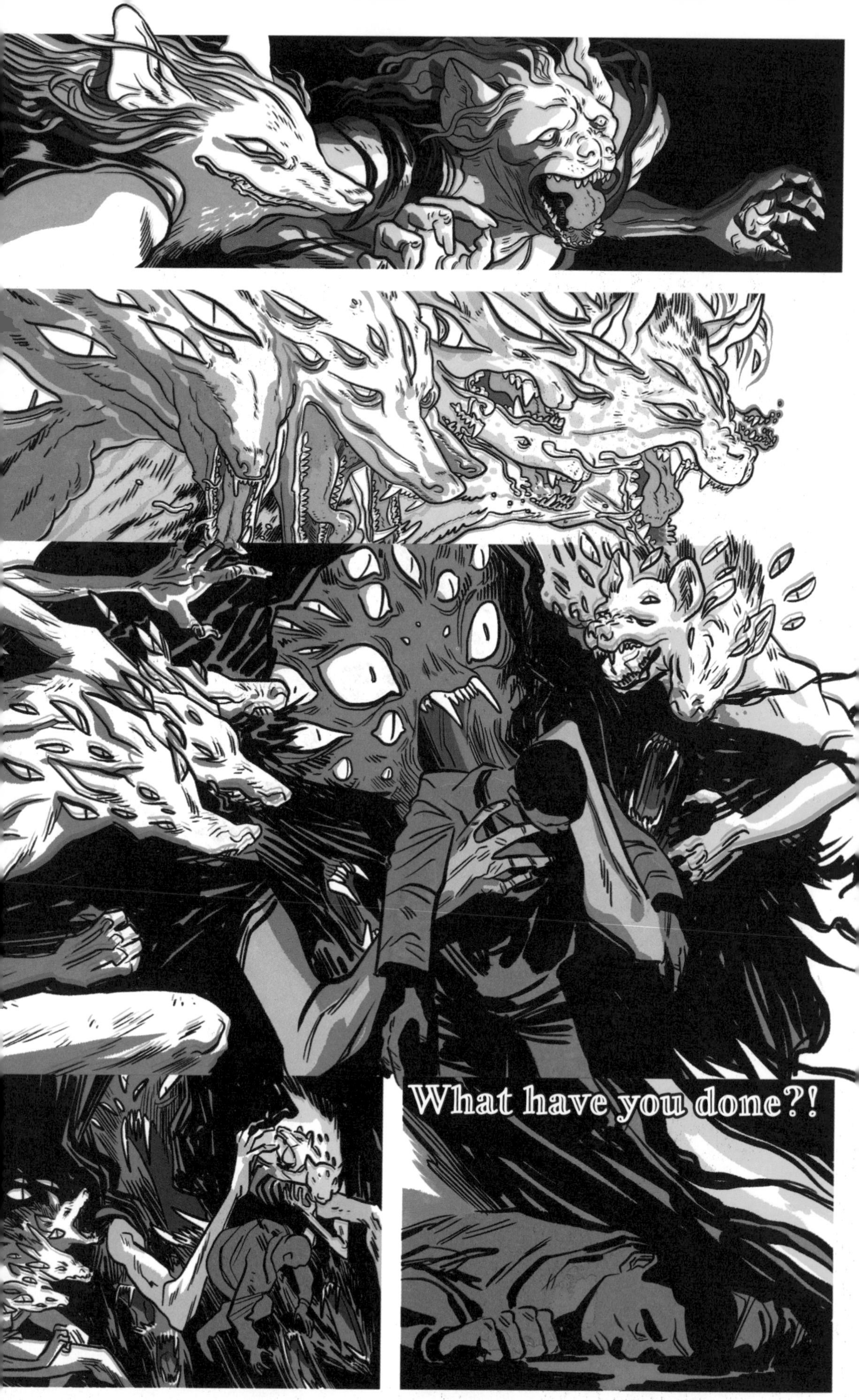
What have you done?!

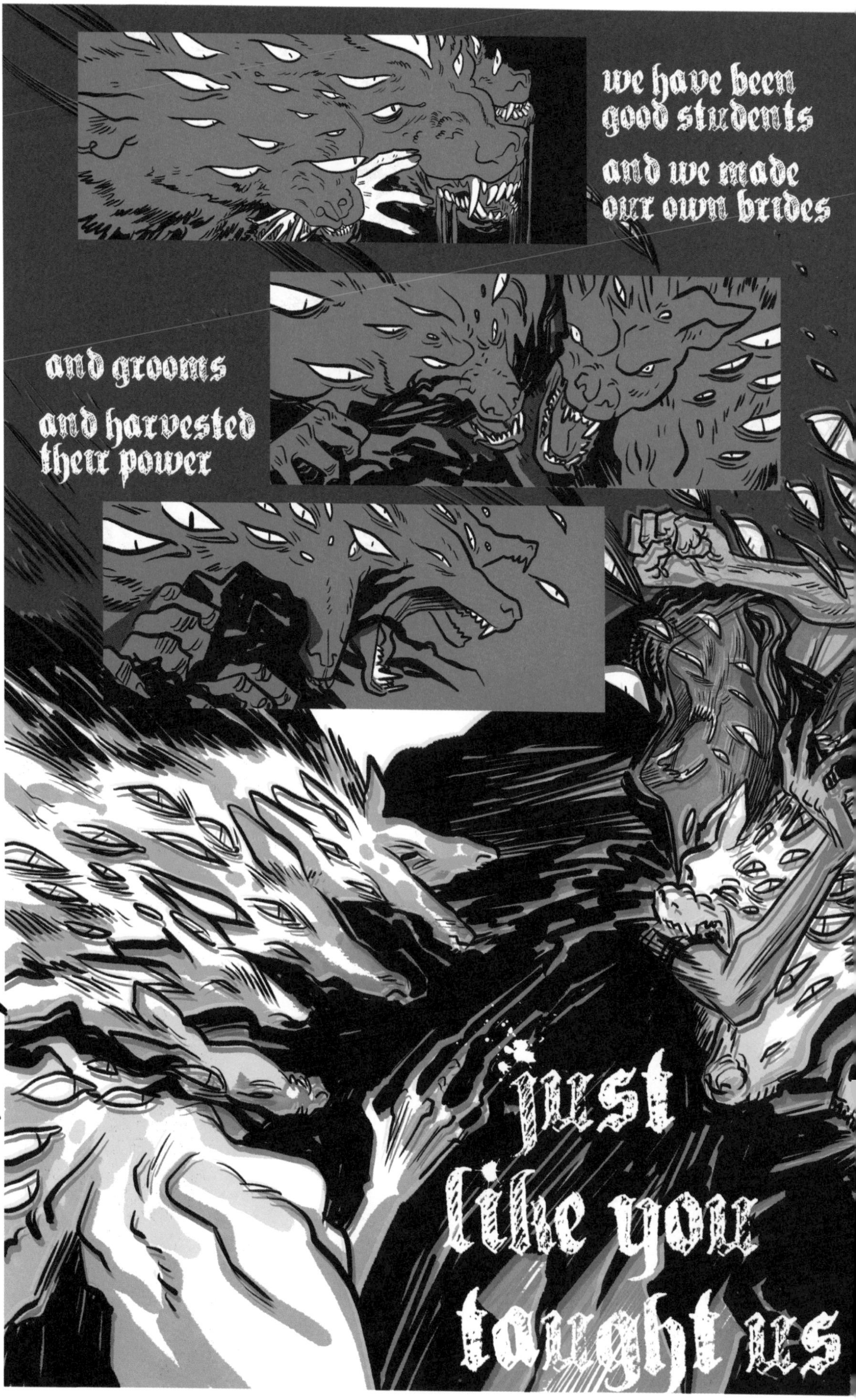
we have been good students
and we made our own brides
and grooms
and harvested their power
just like you taught us

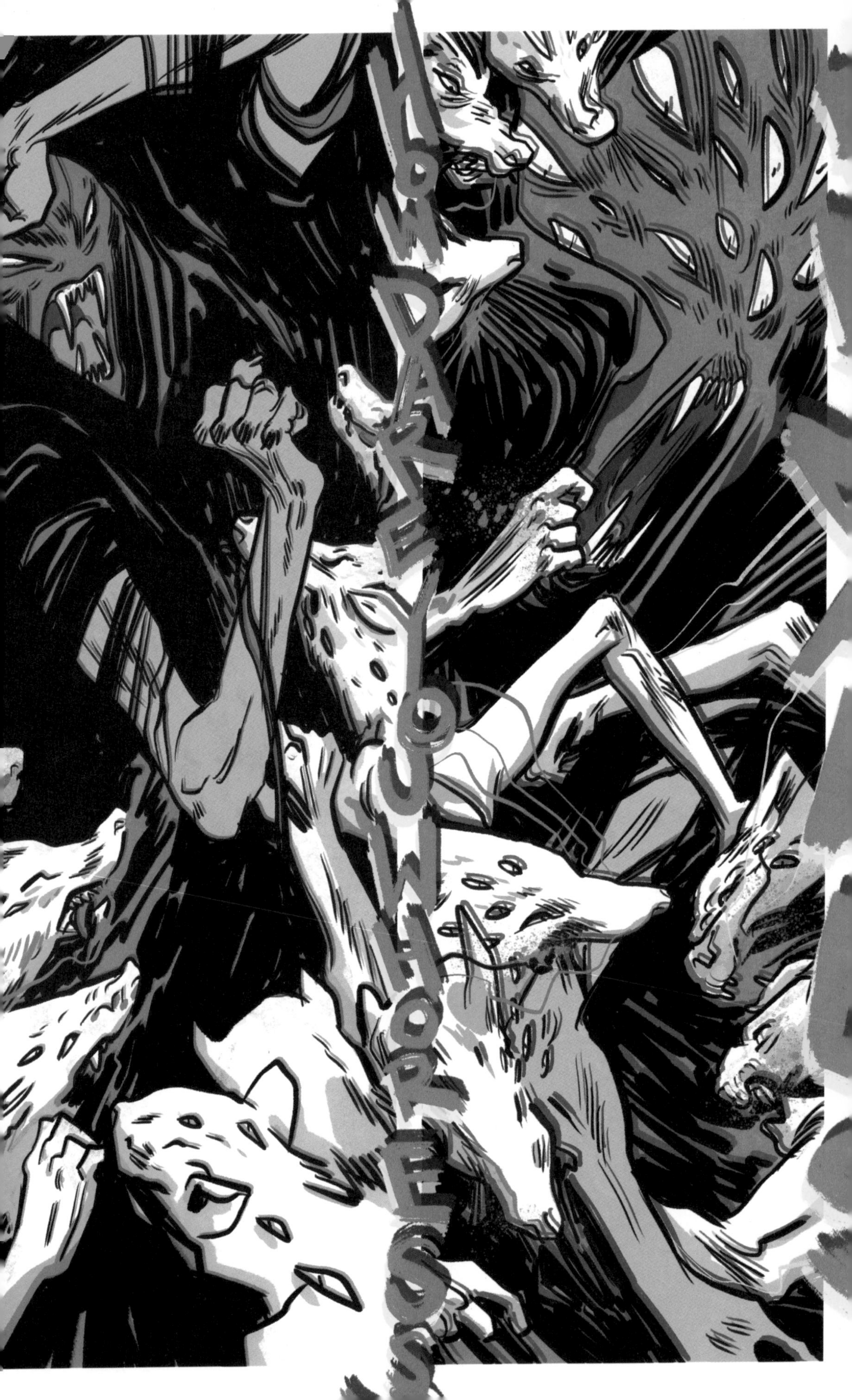
HOW DARE YOU WHORESS

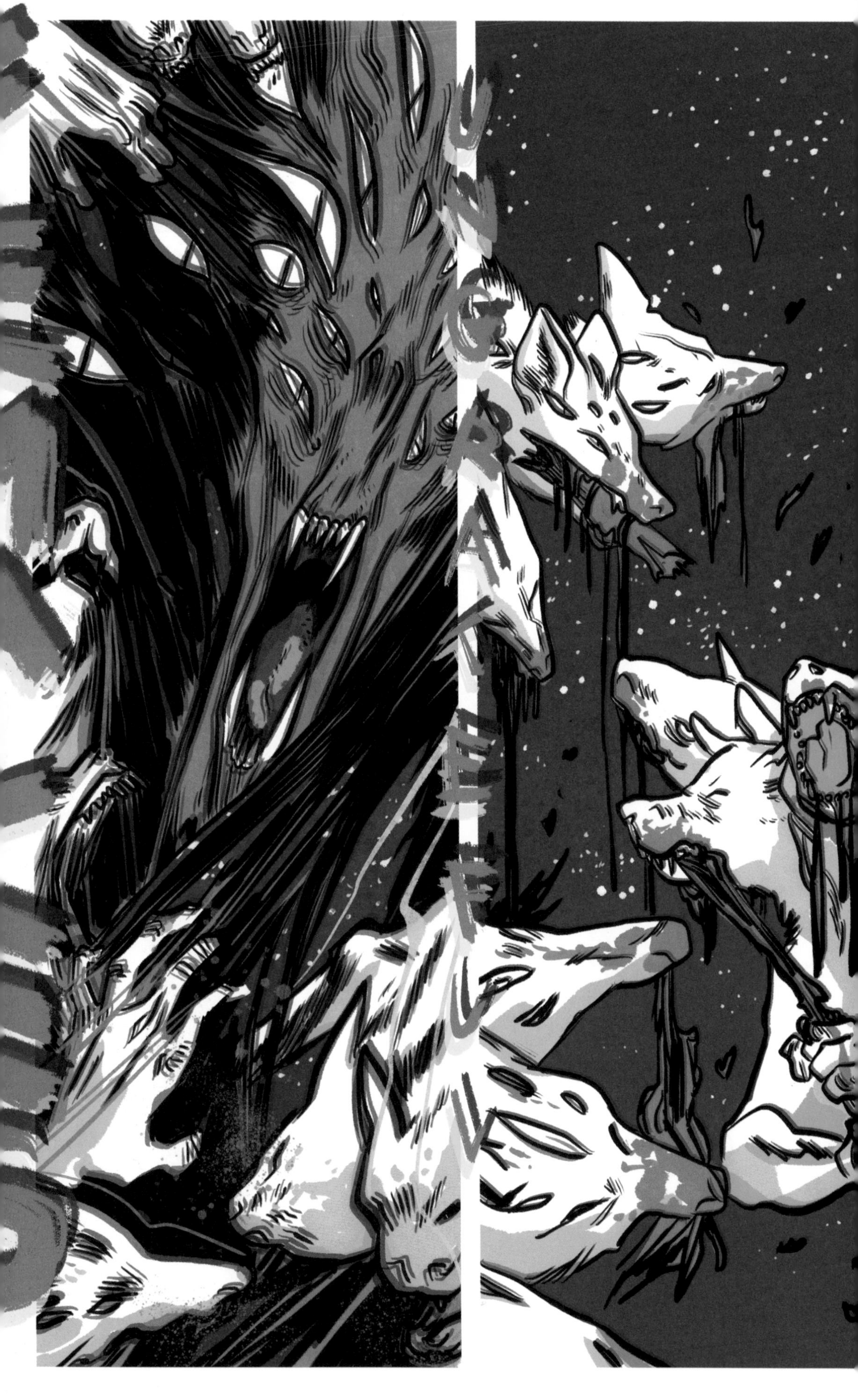

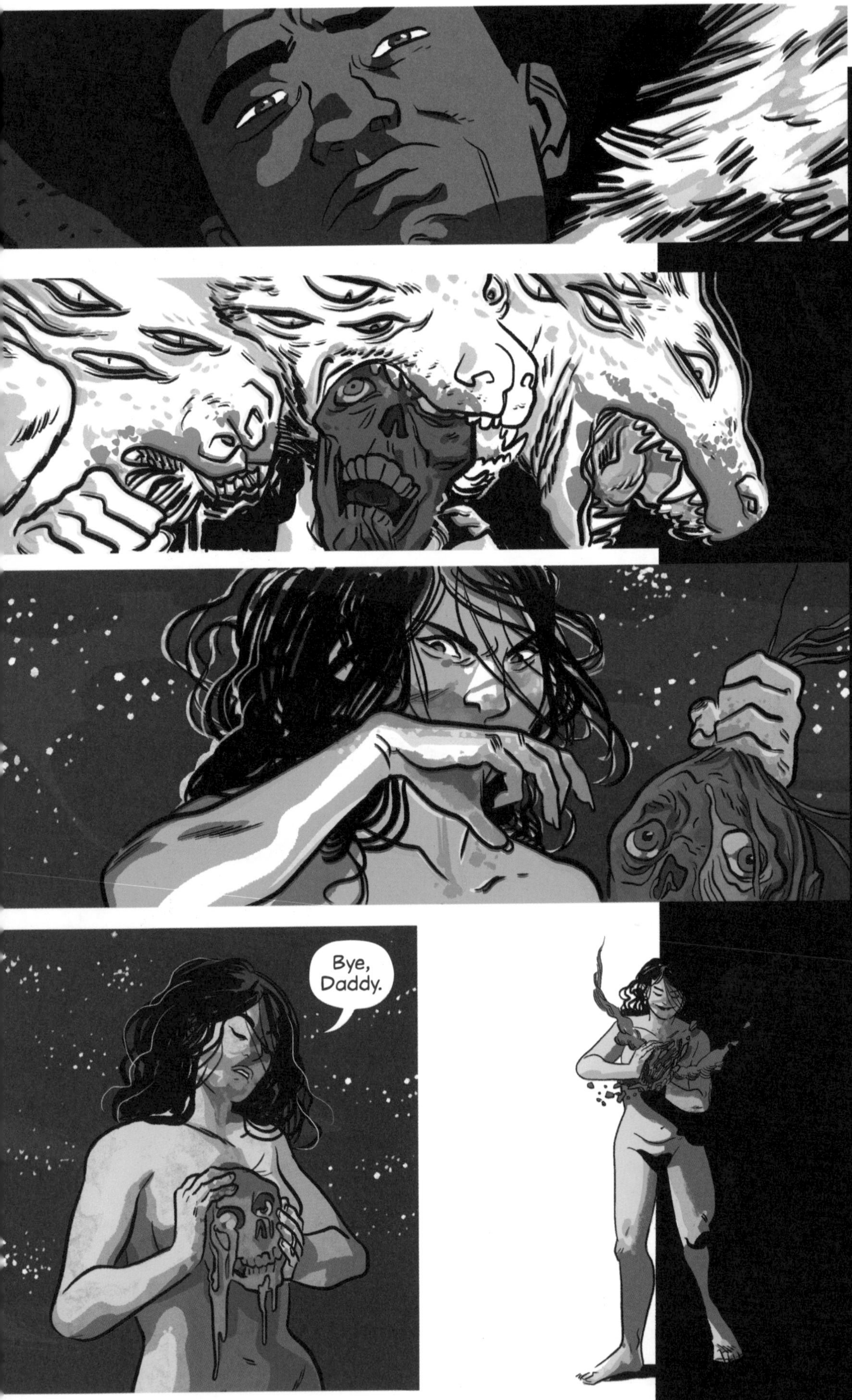
Bye,
Daddy.

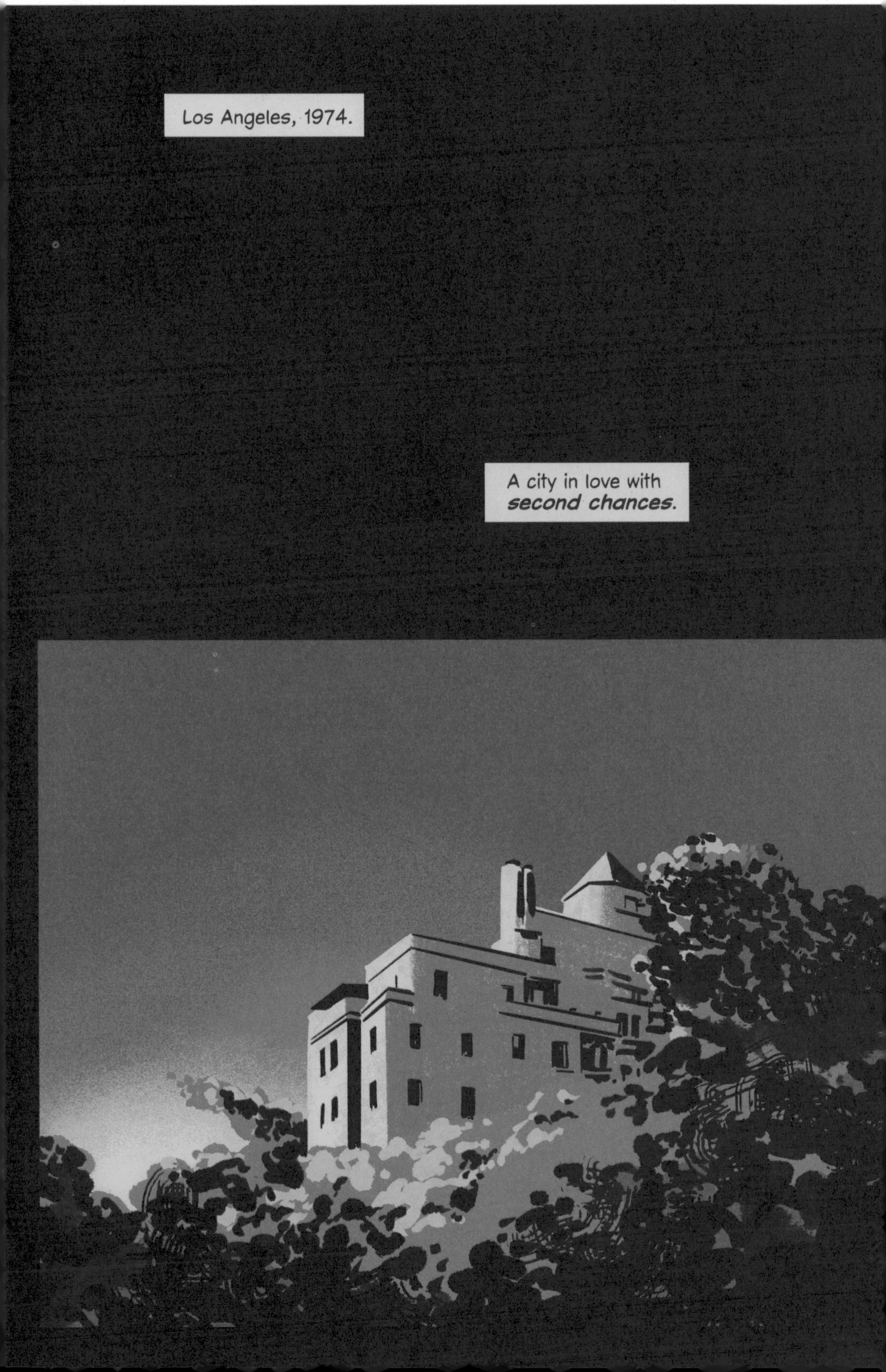
Los Angeles, 1974.
A city in love with *second chances*.

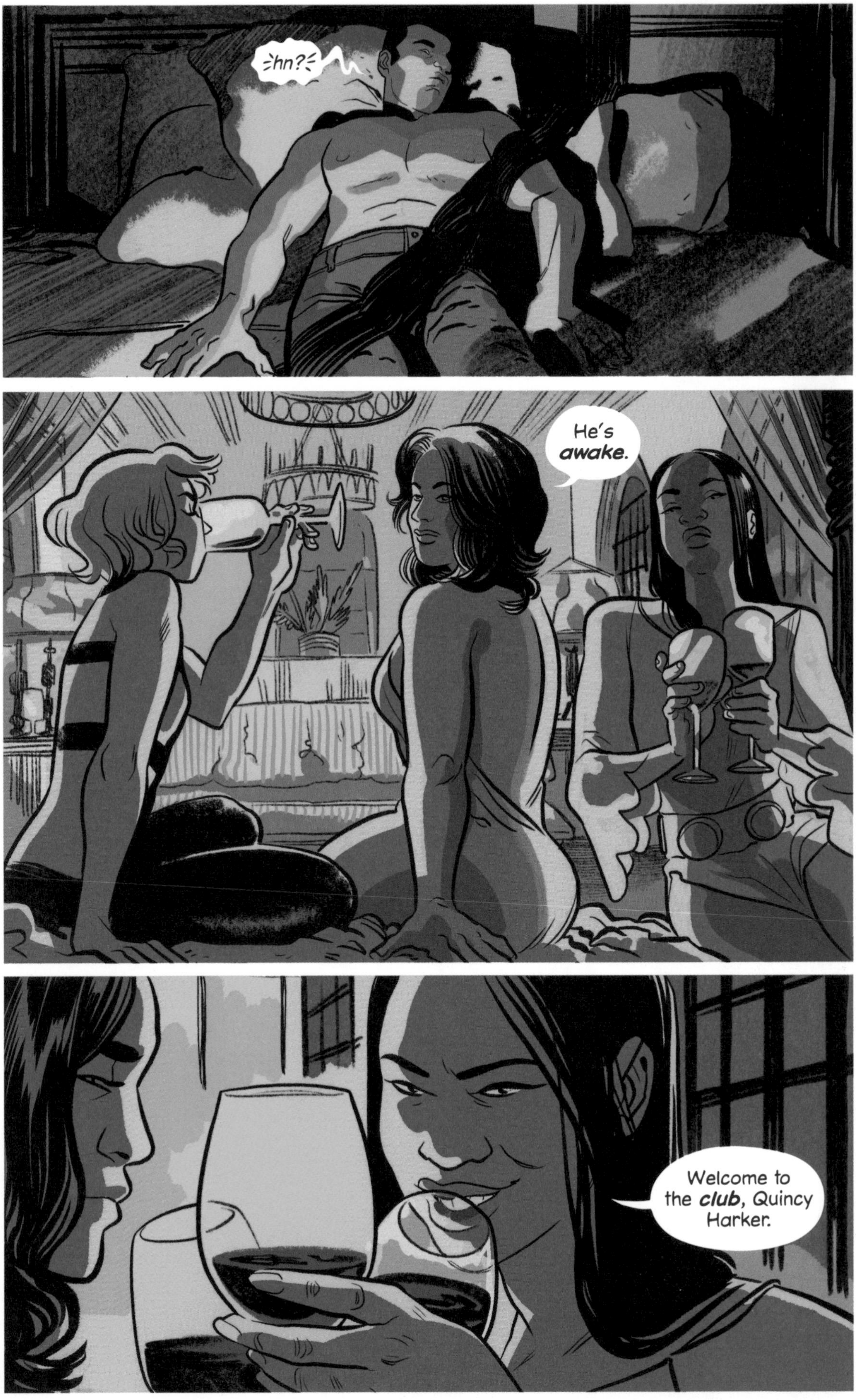
hn?
He's *awake.*
Welcome to the *club,* Quincy Harker.

the end.

Character designs

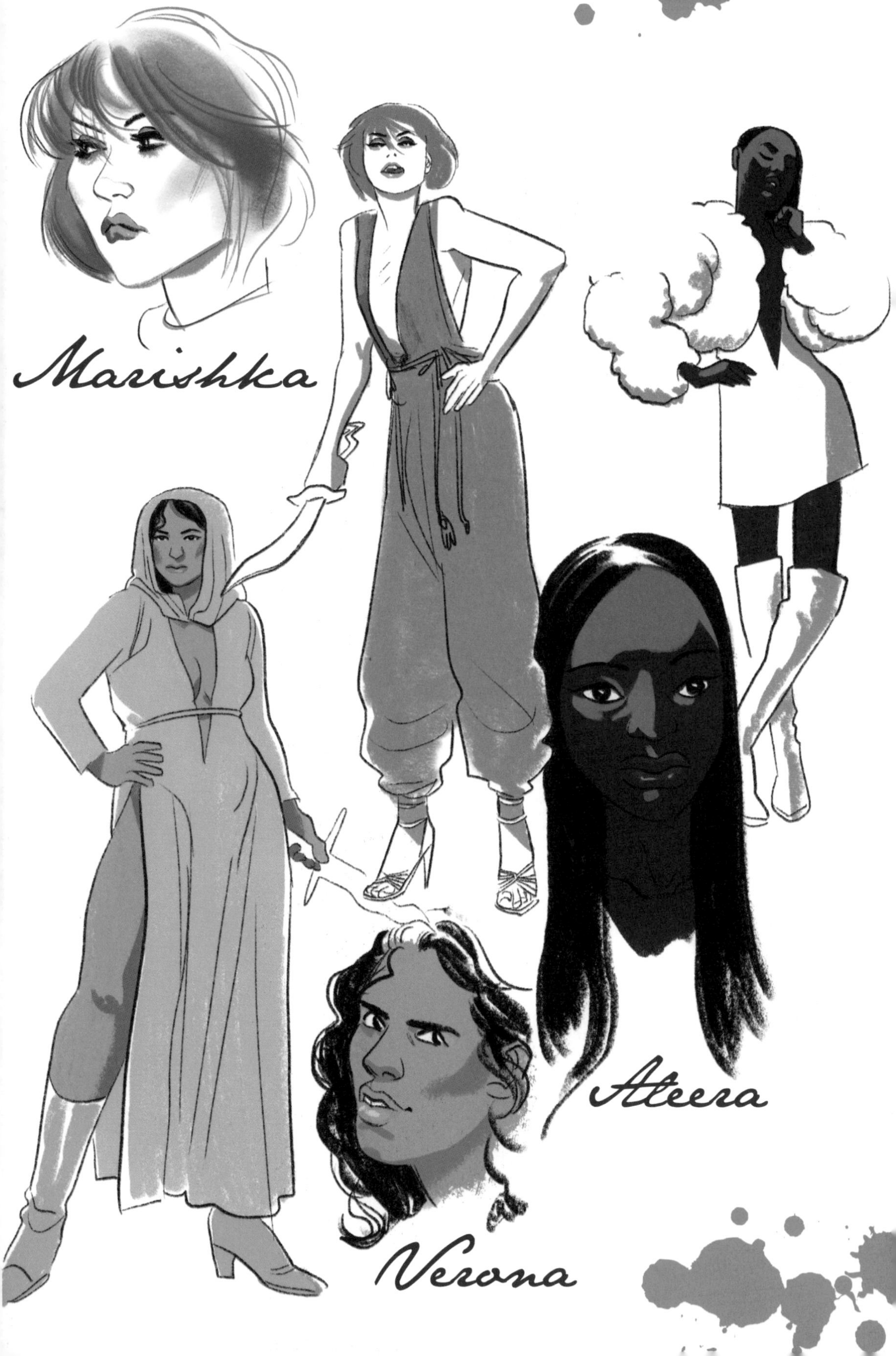
Marishka
Ateera
Verona

Bebe Beauland

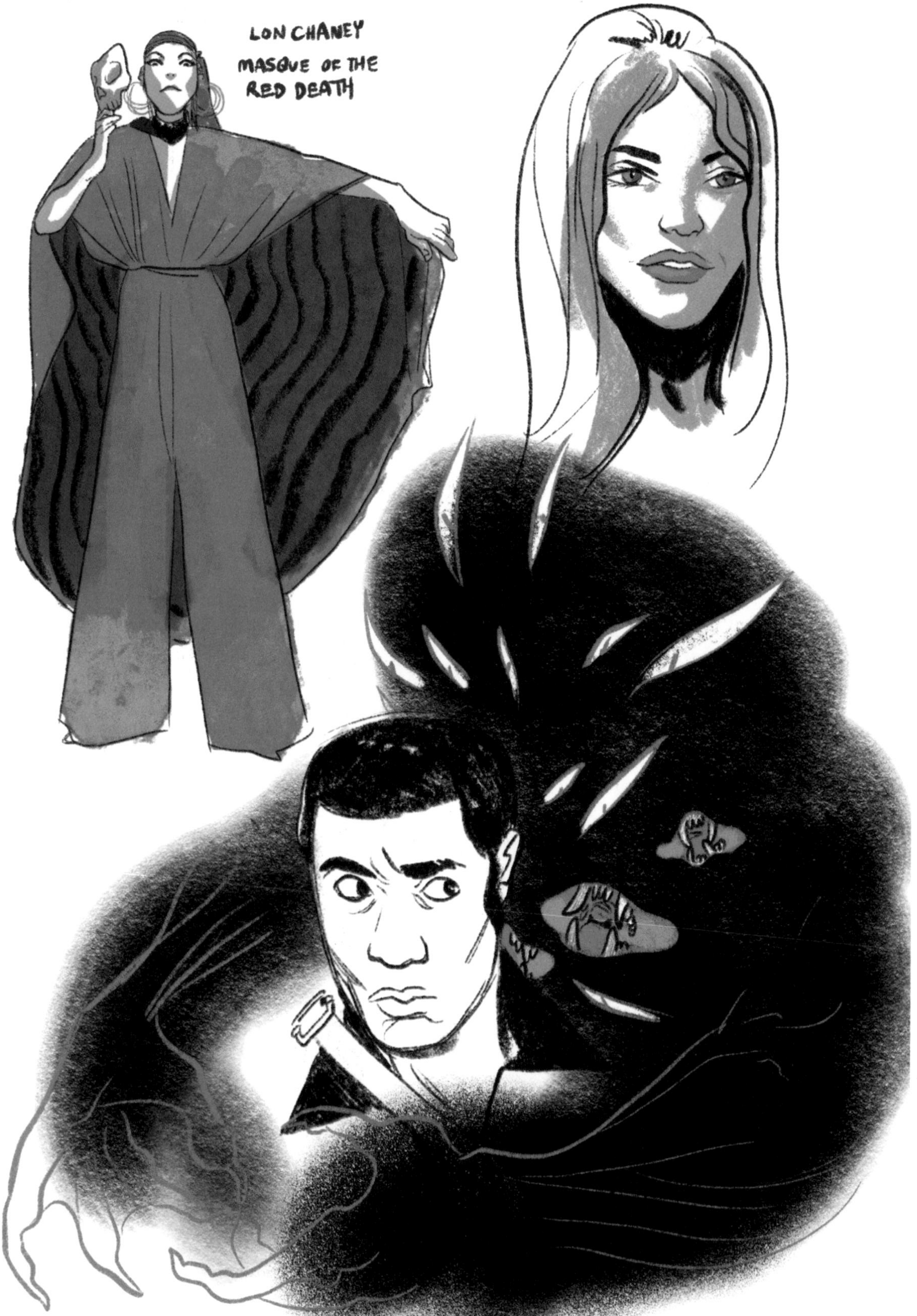
LON CHANEY
MASQUE OF THE
RED DEATH

Quincy Harker

Page design

by Erica Henderson

With this graphic novel, I thought I'd try something new. I'm sure it's in no way groundbreaking, but it's new for me and it was a really useful way to look at the book as a whole. It was basically two things:

1. My layouts were done as spreads, not pages.
2. I colored my layouts as I went.

Let's talk about the first subject. Early on, I was looking at the script and said to Alex, "Hey, we should move this transition from x page to y page because that's where the page turn will be." When that happened, I came to the realization that I no longer have to worry about someone sticking an ad in the middle of my story. We get to determine where each page goes because this is our book.

Let's get back to the page turn. The page turn is literally where you turn the page. In prose, it's an irrelevant idea, but with comics, you're seeing two pages worth of story before you even get to read it because that is how eyes work.

Therefore, if you have a big visual reveal you want to literally hide it on the next page. You want to make sure it always happens on an even (left-hand) page rather than an odd (right-hand) page.

The way we take in a comic book is page turn > spread > page > panel. So why wasn't I looking at the spread every time?

The visual information that you casually take in when you open to a new page is important and I needed to get into the habit of thinking about that. When you get to a new spread, you're immediately given a sense of mood (even if it's the same mood as the one before), you're shown a map of how to get through the page (which can also determine mood with discordant panels, grids, etc) and... all of that is in the color too. So that takes us to point number two.

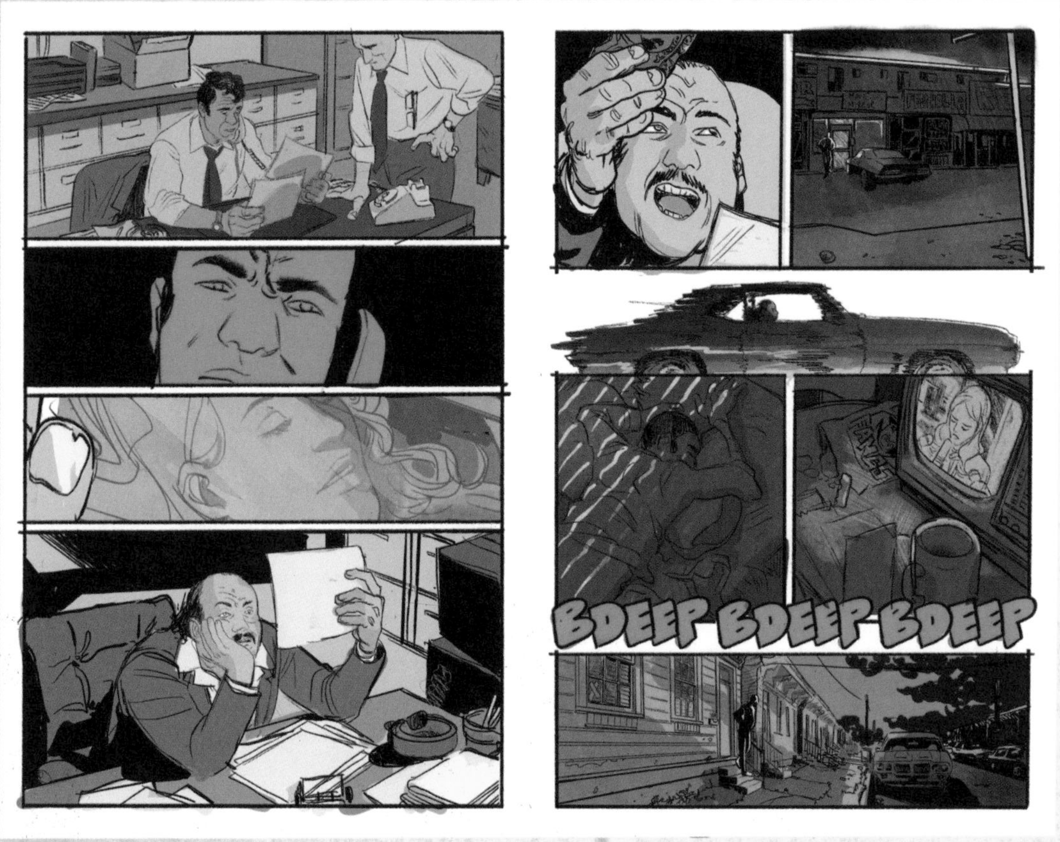
BDEEP BDEEP BDEEP

I appreciate the level of abstraction that comics allows us to work in, as a baseline. It's harder to convincingly go abstract in film because we're experiencing images and sound and the movement of time largely in the same way we would in real life, with our senses. With the written word, a writer can say that a character looks incomprehensible and we have to accept that this person cannot be comprehended. Comics are somewhere in the middle.

I don't feel the need to strive for realism in comics because we're already having to stitch together scenes using one or two drawings and some text. So why try to pretend like we're dealing with real life? All of this is to say that while doing this 1970s neo-noir Dracula book, I did not feel like I needed to work with realistic color.

What's more important to me when it comes to color is the ability to set a tone, and to help guide the reader between panels and scenes. Every setting has it's own color, so if we're bopping back and forth between them, we know where we are. In the page above, we see two almost identical panels of men looking at a sheet of paper. There are a few other visual cues but coloring one as beige and the other an anemic green instantly gives you an idea of what the difference between the two are.

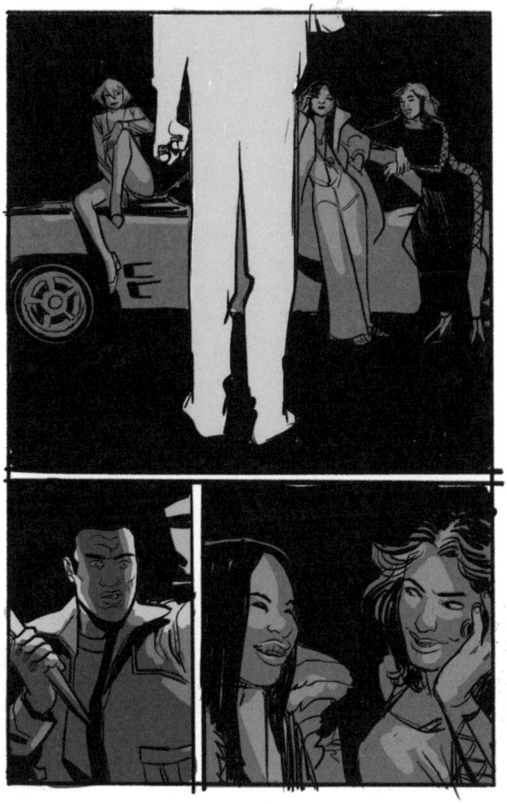

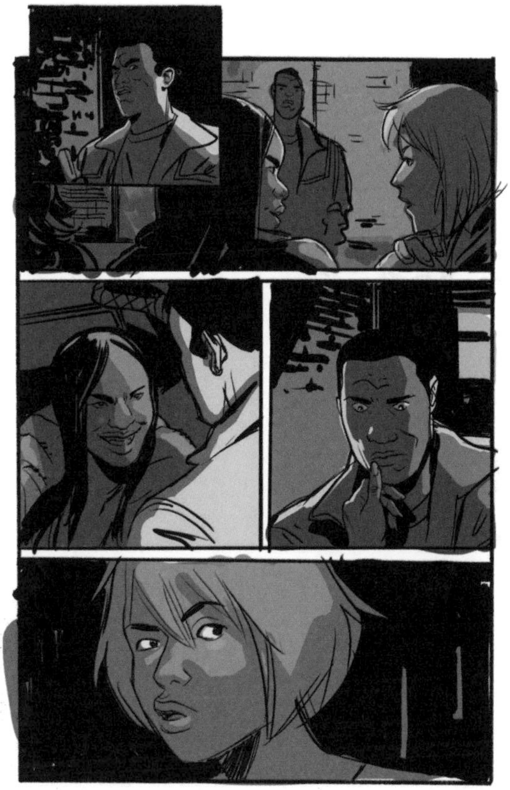

On the first spread posted, Alex gave two pages that basically allow for a moody transition from dusk to night so I could just play with colors that read as different levels of nighttime without just being dark. What was nice about doing this during the pencils/roughs stage is I know that the panel flow will work with these colors. I can plan things based on color rather than trying to make the colors work as the last step.

That's it really. I don't have any greater point to make. I just wanted to let you guys in on my thought processes during the making of this book. I hope you liked it.

– Erica.

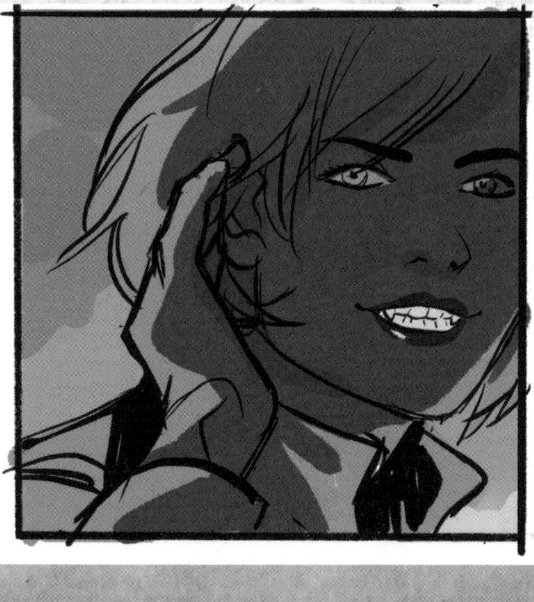

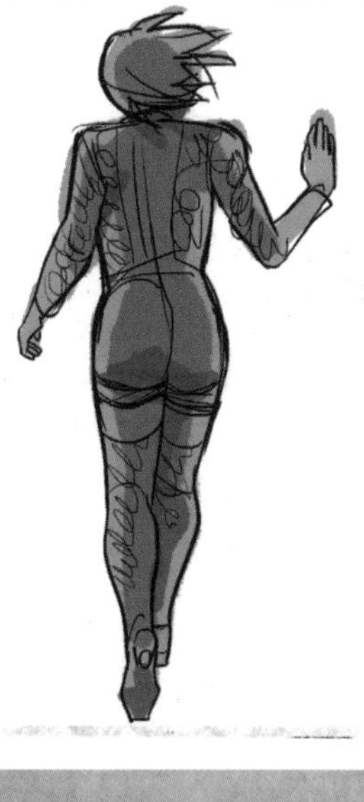

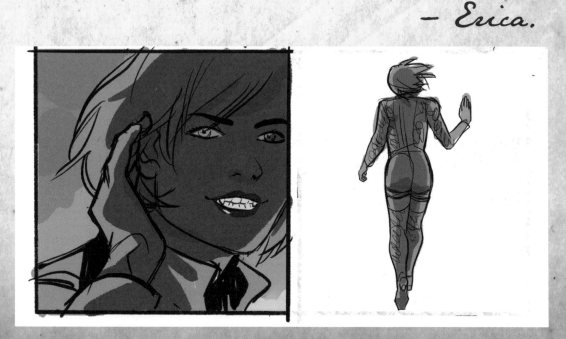

On monsters
by Alex de Campi

The petty hill I will die on is that Dracula should never be handsome. Oh, it's easier if he's pretty. Then it's love; these poor maids who are his victims take one look at his face and can't believe something so evil could look so nice. It's like making your hero a lone wolf, or killing his family to justify his vengeance. It makes the storytelling easier, building your tales on the back of lovelorn dead women.

But I'm not in the business of ease.

The Brides have always fascinated me, in a very different way than they could fascinate male writers, because I know them. They interest me in the way Melania Trump does, in the way Georgina Chapman Weinstein does. In the way that every woman, at least once in her life, wonders, "Could I just...?" Most of us could never go through with it, of course. But some do.

What if the Brides did? What if Dracula wasn't a handsome Romanian prince, but a nameless, faceless ancient terror? What would you trade for a life of enormous wealth, released from the cruel rigors of ageing into a state of eternal beauty? How much would you be willing to fake, and for how long?

Of course the deal is bad, and the monster turns out to be even more of a monster than you suspect when you make it. But again, this is no surprise to most women. And ask any abuse survivor, you have to become a little bit of a monster yourself to escape it.

On the one hand this is just a fun, overheated pulp fantasia about terror in the night, but being a Brides of Dracula story, you can also read it as about the unchecked predatory actions of powerful men and the compromises and tragedies of the women who think it'll be different for them than for all the other women beforehand. Why does a creature so old take brides so young? Why indeed...

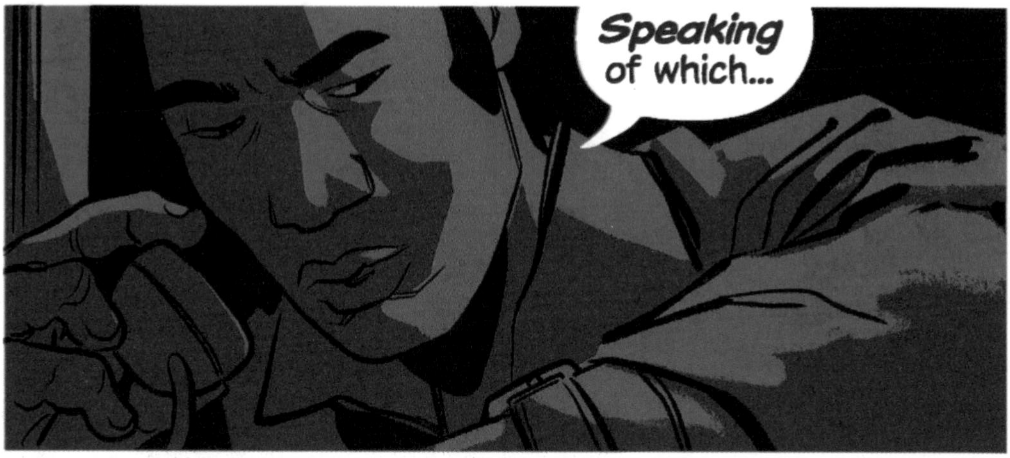
Speaking of which...

It's wrong to encase a monster in flesh, to give it a face. It belittles the darkness, makes it smaller, dimmer, to decant it into the image of one particular man. I come to each book with a definite aesthetic. For *DRACULA, MOTHERF**KER,* it was using a specific flatness and abstract two-dimensionality to push the expression of man-as-monster in ways that could only be done in sequential art: blending sensibilities from Japanese Superflat art and things like the late-1960s psychedelic liquid light projections of the Joshua Light Show and the strict abstractions of Op Art, to the works of Klimt that we reference in the book's 1889 prologue.

This was specifically to characterize Dracula as an unknowable Other. A large portion of this came from the way horror is portrayed in Japanese anime, from the witches in *Madoka Magica* to Alucard going incorporeal in *Hellsing* to Pride in *FMA: Brotherhood.* Allowing evil to have an inchoate form gives the reader space to put the faces of their choosing to it, to fit it to monsters that they have known.

I also have a lot of feelings about the modernization of Gothic horror. It's always a dark-haired man in a funny cape in London, or some old castle, somewhere else that has old roots, and it never really works. Retire your fog machines, my friends, and think again about what the heart of Gothic horror is, rather than simply what its accessories were 125 years ago. Make something new out of the old.

That's why the book is set in Los Angeles which, *Count Yorba* aside, is a vastly under-used location for vampire horror tales. Los Angeles can be, for me, a strange, rootless, isolating city, full of lonely, vulnerable people in the night, people who might not be missed for a long time if they vanish. If you disappeared, how long until someone would know? A day? A week?

That's how we express it through Quincy Harker, who roams the city after dark, waiting for it to bring out its dead so he can immortalize them for newspaper readers' prurient interest. (No part of the book occurs during daytime. We don't make it obvious, but it's all nocturnes.)

Quincy Harker, obviously, comes... well, I won't say directly from Bram Stoker's *Dracula*. He's more of a riff on it. In the book, he's Jonathan and Mina's kid, and I remember re-reading *Dracula* and snorting with laughter when I got to him because it's the most accidentally black name in white literature since Percy Jackson. That's another part of the modernization: wanting to seamlessly blend the world I see in my friends group into this overwhelmingly white tradition without it feeling like a statement. It just is.

Erica has been an absolute dream to work with. She brings so, so much to the book, from her expert visual storytelling skills and her experimental, wildly exciting use of colour in this story to her appreciation of my Demi Moore jokes.

One of the joys of this book was how we unrepentantly played with colour, from black and white photos to darkroom reds to the very *Zabriskie Point* house explosion at the end. It's Sean Phillips' fault: he warned us that the paper on these books soaks up colour like nobody's business, so we just cranked everything up to 11 and went for it. There are so many of her pages I could talk about in this regard. Page 31, a nocturne with chartreuse silhouettes on a cobalt background, so striking I gasped: the palette, straight out of Robert McGinnis pulp covers. Any of the darkroom sequences, with their deliberately restricted carmine light. The discovery of the body in the LA River. All of it.

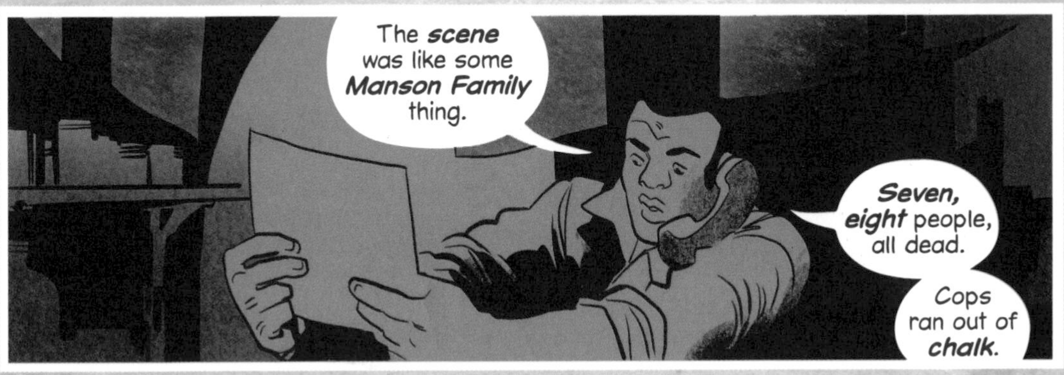
The *scene* was like some *Manson Family* thing.
Seven, eight people, all dead.
Cops ran out of *chalk*.

We worked very much like a jazz band, passing ideas back and forth. I wrote a very complete script (as always) and then I gave her carte blanche to change any part of it she wanted. And she did, and she improved it from the script, which is right and proper. A script is only ever a beginning, never a destination. She sent me colour roughs (reproduced in her process section, previously) and I lettered on those. Then she hand-drew SFX where I had temped in the fonts, as below.

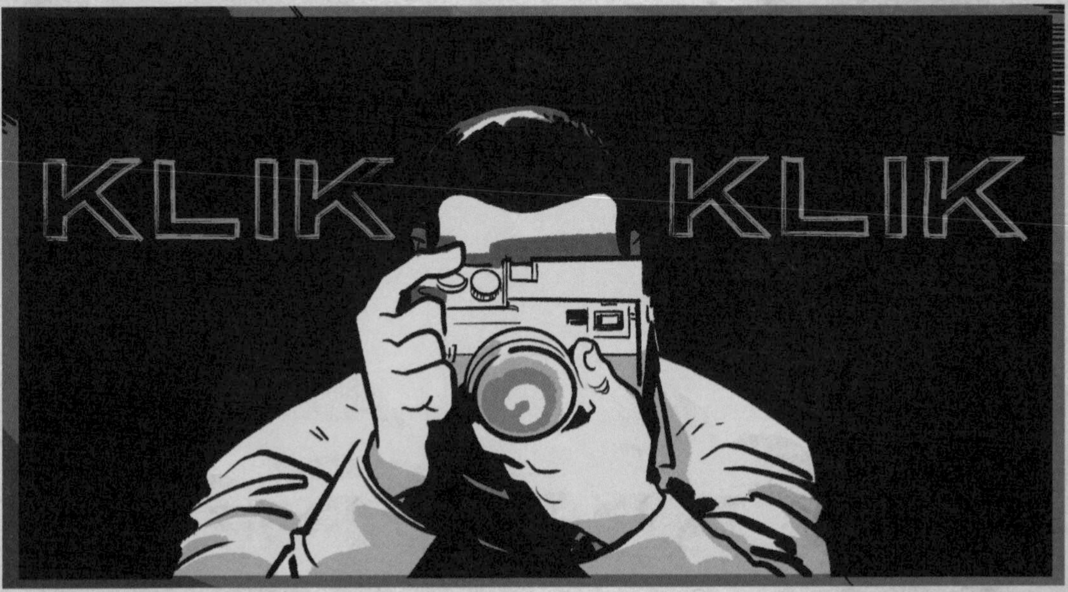
KLIK
KLIK

She finalized her pages; I tweaked the letters approximately a billion times; and finally we stopped and handed the book to Image. (A work of art is never finished; only abandoned.) For me, this book was a playground, a way of being serious and unserious at the same time. I'd been feeling like my style had been getting perhaps too documentary lately, and this was an attempt to see what the other direction felt like. I hope you enjoy it.

— Alex

PAGE 12. FOUR PANELS, SAME SIZE, ALL FULL WIDTH OF PAGE

PANEL 1. Full width of page. A NEWSPAPER PHOTO EDITOR at desk. Mussed, but middle-aged White guy (Walter Matthau in *Pelham 123*) sitting at his desk, with a slightly younger, more tidy white guy standing next to him, hands on hips (the Editor, calling the shots). Night desk, tired, full ashtrays. Cool colours. Venetian blinds, windows behind, maybe some neon creeping in through the blinds. NOTE: We never see full daylight in this entire story, it's either night, dusk/dawn, or inside without real windows.

PHOTO EDITOR: Sorry, Quincy.

PHOTO EDITOR (linked): Bebe Beauland's making a statement at 3pm today.

PANEL 2. Full width of page. The red of the developing room. A shellshocked Quincy, standing, centered in CU, holding the phone.

PHOTO EDITOR (from phone): Paper wants to be respectful of her trauma.

PHOTO EDITOR (from phone): Boss says we can do $25 for the set, non-exclusive.

PANEL 3. Full width of page. The photo image of Very Dead Bebe Beauland. Someone's holding it. White hands.

NO DIALOGUE

PANEL 4. Full width of page. Echo the image in Panel 1, but this office is shabby as hell, in a basement, and you KNOW it smells. A TABLOID EDITOR frowns at the photo he holds. (It's the one in Panel 3 but we only see it from the back). Is he smoking a cigar? He can smoke a cigar. He may also have a mullet and 'tache.

TABLOID EDITOR: You coulda at least pulled her skirt up so we see some leg, Harker.

TABLOID EDITOR: I coulda given you double for leg.

TABLOID EDITOR: Triple for boobs.

IMAGE COMICS, INC.

Robert Kirkman—Chief Operating Officer
Erik Larsen—Chief Financial Officer
Todd McFarlane—President
Marc Silvestri—Chief Executive Officer
Jim Valentino—Vice President
Eric Stephenson—Publisher/Chief Creative Officer
Jeff Boison—Director of Sales & Publishing Planning
Jeff Stang—Director of Direct Market Sales
Kat Salazar—Director of PR & Marketing
Drew Gill—Cover Editor
Heather Doornink—Production Director
Nicole Lapalme—Controller

IMAGECOMICS.COM